HANNAH SNOW'S LIFE was perfect . . . until the notes started appearing. Notes in her own handwriting, warning her of the danger that was coming.

Dead before seventeen.

Therapy was supposed to help. But what came out instead were memories of another time, another life. And of a stranger who tore her world apart . . . a vampire who killed a village in his rage. Until, in the eyes of a dying human girl, he recognized his soulmate.

Now the stranger is back. He has searched for her, waiting for her to be reborn. He is Thierry, a Lord of the Night World—and nothing in heaven or hell will keep him from his soulmate again. But if her destiny is death, can even Thierry's love protect her?

SOULMATE

THE NIGHT WORLD
SERIES

· · · · · · · · · · · · · · · · · · ·

NIGHT WORLD · BOOK SIX

SOULMATE

L. J. SMITH

SIMON PULSE

NEW YORK   LONDON   TORONTO   SYDNEY   NEW DELHI

SIMON PULSE

An imprint of Simon & Schuster Children's Publishing Division

1230 Avenue of the Americas, New York, New York 10020

This Simon Pulse hardcover edition April 2017

Text copyright © 1997 by Lisa J. Smith

Cover illustration copyright © 2017 by Neal Williams

Endpaper art of flowers, heart, and sunburst respectively copyright © 2017 by Liliya Shlapak, Nattle, and Ezepov Dmitry/Shutterstock.com

Endpaper art of ornamental flourishes copyright © 2017 by Thinkstock

All rights reserved, including the right of reproduction in whole or in part in any form.

SIMON PULSE and colophon are registered trademarks of Simon & Schuster, Inc.

NIGHT WORLD is a trademark of Lisa J. Smith

For information about special discounts for bulk purchases, please contact Simon & Schuster Special Sales at 1-866-506-1949 or business@simonandschuster.com.

The Simon & Schuster Speakers Bureau can bring authors to your live event.

For more information or to book an event contact the Simon & Schuster Speakers Bureau at 1-866-248-3049 or visit our website at www.simonspeakers.com.

Cover designed by Regina Flath

Interior designed by Mike Rosamilia

The text of this book was set in Adobe Garamond.

Manufactured in the United States of America

2 4 6 8 10 9 7 5 3 1

Library of Congress Control Number 2016948193

ISBN 978-1-4814-8940-9 (hc)

ISBN 978-1-4814-8941-6 (eBook)

For Marion Foster Divola

CHAPTER 1

The werewolves broke in while Hannah Snow was in the psychologist's office.

She was there for the obvious reason. "I think I'm going insane," she said quietly as soon as she sat down.

"And what makes you think that?" The psychologist's voice was neutral, soothing.

Hannah swallowed.

Okay, she thought. Lay it on the line. Skip the paranoid feeling of being followed and the ultra-paranoid feeling that someone was trying to kill her, ignore the dreams that woke her up screaming. Go straight to the *really* weird stuff.

"I write notes," she said flatly.

"Notes." The therapist nodded, tapping a pencil against his lips. Then as the silence stretched out: "Uh, and that bothers you?"

"Yes." She added in a jagged rush, "Everything used to

be so perfect. I mean, I had my whole life under control. I'm a senior at Sacajawea High. I have nice friends; I have good grades. I even have a scholarship from Utah State for next year. And now it's all falling apart . . . because of me. Because I'm going *crazy.*"

"Because you write notes?" the psychologist said, puzzled. "Um, poison pen letters, compulsive memo taking . . . ?"

"Notes like these." Hannah leaned forward in her chair and dropped a handful of crumpled scraps of paper on his desk. Then she looked away miserably as he read them.

He seemed like a nice guy—and surprisingly young for a shrink, she thought. His name was Paul Winfield—"Call me Paul," he'd said—and he had red hair and analytical blue eyes. He looked as if he might have both a sense of humor and a temper.

And he likes me, Hannah thought. She'd seen the flicker of appreciation in his eyes when he'd opened the front door and found her standing silhouetted against the flaming Montana sunset.

And then she'd seen that appreciation change to utter blankness, startled neutrality, when she stepped inside and her face was revealed.

It didn't matter. People usually gave Hannah two looks, one for the long, straight fair hair and the clear gray eyes . . . and one for the birthmark.

It slanted diagonally beneath her left cheekbone, pale strawberry color, as if someone had dipped a finger in blusher and then drawn it gently across Hannah's face. It was permanent—the doctors had removed it twice with lasers, and it had come back both times.

Hannah was used to the stares it got her.

Paul cleared his throat suddenly, startling her. She looked back at him.

"'Dead before seventeen,'" he read out loud, thumbing through the scraps of paper. "'Remember the Three Rivers—DO NOT throw this note away.' 'The cycle *can* be broken.' 'It's almost May—you know what happens then.'" He picked up the last scrap. "And this one just says, 'He's coming.'"

He smoothed the papers and looked at Hannah. "What do they mean?"

"I don't know."

"You don't know?"

"I didn't write them," Hannah said through her teeth.

Paul blinked and tapped his pencil faster. "But you said you *did* write them—"

"It's my handwriting. I admit that," Hannah said. Now that she had gotten started, the words came out in gasping bursts, unstoppable. "And I find them in places where nobody else could put them . . . in my sock drawer, inside my pillowcase. This morning I woke up and I was holding that last one in my fist. But *I still don't write them.*"

Paul waved his pencil triumphantly. "I see. You don't *remember* writing them."

"I don't remember because I didn't *do* it. I would never write things like that. They're all nonsense."

"Well." *Tap. Tap.* "I guess that depends. 'It's almost May'— what happens in May?"

"May first is my birthday."

"That's, what, a week from now? A week and a day. And you'll be . . . ?"

Hannah let out her breath. "Seventeen."

She saw the psychologist pick up one of the scraps—she didn't need to ask which one.

Dead before seventeen, she thought.

"You're young to be graduating," Paul said.

"Yeah. My mom taught me at home when I was a kid, and they put me in first grade instead of kindergarten."

Paul nodded, and she thought she could see him thinking *overachiever.*

"Have you ever"—he paused delicately—"had any thoughts about suicide?"

"*No.* Never. I would never do anything like that."

"Hmm . . ." Paul frowned, staring at the notes. There was a long silence and Hannah looked around the room.

It was decorated like a psychologist's office, even though it was just part of a house. Out here in central Montana, with miles between ranches, towns were few and far between. So were psychologists—which was why Hannah was here. Paul Winfield was the only one available.

There were diplomas on the walls; books and impersonal knickknacks were in the bookcase. A carved wooden elephant. A semi-dead plant. A silver-framed photograph. There was even an official-looking couch. And am I going to lie on that? Hannah thought. I don't *think* so.

Paper rustled as Paul pushed a note aside. Then he said gently, "Do you feel that someone else is trying to hurt you?"

Hannah shut her eyes.

Of course she felt that someone was trying to hurt her. That was part of being paranoid, wasn't it? It proved she was crazy.

"Sometimes I have the feeling I'm being followed," she said at last in almost a whisper.

"By . . . ?"

"I don't know." Then she opened her eyes and said flatly, "Something weird and supernatural that's out to get me. And I have dreams about the apocalypse."

Paul blinked. "The—apoc . . ."

"The end of the world. At least I guess that's what it is. Some huge battle that's coming: some giant horrible *ultimate* fight. Between the forces of . . ." She saw how he was staring at her. She looked away and went on resignedly. "Good." She held out one hand. "And evil." She held out the other. Then both hands went limp and she put them in her lap. "So I'm crazy, right?"

"No, no, no." He fumbled with the pencil, then patted his pocket. "Do you happen to have a cigarette?"

She glanced at him in disbelief, and he flinched. "No, of course you don't. What am I saying? It's a filthy habit. I quit last week."

Hannah opened her mouth, closed it, then spoke slowly. "Look, Doctor—I mean, Paul. I'm here because I don't *want* to be crazy. I just want to be *me* again. I want to graduate with my class. I want to have a great summer horseback riding with my best friend, Chess. And next year I want to go to Utah State and study dinosaurs and maybe find a duckbill nest site of my own. I want my *life* back. But if you can't help me . . ."

She stopped and gulped. She almost never cried; it was the ultimate loss of control. But now she couldn't help it. She could feel warmth spill out of her eyes and trace down her cheeks to tickle her chin. Humiliated, she wiped away the teardrops as Paul peered around for a tissue. She sniffed.

"I'm sorry," he said. He'd found a box of Kleenex, but now he left it to come and stand beside her. His eyes weren't analytical now; they were blue and boyish as he tentatively squeezed her hand. "I'm sorry, Hannah. It sounds awful. But I'm sure I *can* help you. We'll get to the bottom of it. You'll see, by summertime you'll be graduating with Utah State and riding the duckbills, just like always." He smiled to show it was a joke. "All this will be behind you."

"You really think?"

He nodded. Then he seemed to realize he was standing and holding a patient's hand: not a very professional position. He let go hastily. "Maybe you've guessed; you're sort of my first client. Not that I'm not trained—I was in the top ten percent of my class. So. Now." He patted his pockets, came up with the pencil, and stuck it in his mouth. He sat down. "Let's start with the first time you remember having one of these dreams. When—"

He broke off as chimes sounded somewhere inside the house. The doorbell.

He looked flustered. "Who would be . . ." He glanced at a clock in the bookcase and shook his head. "Sorry, this should only take a minute. Just make yourself comfortable until I get back."

"Don't answer it," Hannah said.

She didn't know why she said it. All she knew was that the sound of the doorbell had sent chills running through her and that right now her heart was pounding and her hands and feet were tingling.

Paul looked briefly startled, then he gave her a gentle reassuring smile. "I don't think it's the apocalypse at the door, Hannah. We'll talk about these feelings of apprehension when I get back." He touched her shoulder lightly as he left the room.

Hannah sat listening. He was right, of course. There was nothing at all menacing about a doorbell. It was her own craziness.

She leaned back in the soft contoured chair and looked around the room again, trying to relax.

It's all in my head. The psychologist is going to help me. . . .

At that instant the window across the room exploded.

CHAPTER 2

Hannah found herself on her feet. Her awareness was fragmented and understanding came to her in pieces because she simply couldn't take in the whole situation at once. It was too bizarre.

At first she simply thought of a bomb. The explosion was that loud. Then she realized that something had come *in* the window, that it had come flying through the glass. And that it was in the room with her now, crouching among the broken shards of windowpane.

Even then, she couldn't identify it. It was too incongruous; her mind refused to recognize the shape immediately. Something pretty big—something dark, it offered. A body like a dog's but set higher, with longer legs. Yellow eyes.

And then, as if the right lens had suddenly clicked in front of her eyes, she saw it clearly.

A wolf. There was a big black *wolf* in the room with her.

It was a gorgeous animal, rangy and muscular, with ebony-colored fur and a white streak on its throat like a bolt of lightning. It was looking at her fixedly, with an almost human expression.

Escaped from Yellowstone, Hannah thought dazedly. The naturalists were reintroducing wolves to the park, weren't they? It couldn't be wild; Ryan Harden's great-grandpa had bragged for years about killing the last wolf in Amador County when he was a boy.

Anyway, she told herself, wolves don't attack people. They never attack people. A single wolf would never attack a full-grown teenager.

And all the time her conscious mind was thinking this, something deeper was making her move.

It made her back up slowly, never taking her eyes off the wolf, until she felt the bookcase behind her.

There's something you need to get, a voice in her mind was whispering to her. It wasn't like the voice of another person, but it wasn't exactly like her own mental voice, either. It was a voice like a dark cool wind: competent and rather bleak. Something you saw on a shelf earlier, it said.

In an impossibly graceful motion, from eight feet away, the wolf leaped.

There was no time to be scared. Hannah saw a bushy, flowing black arc coming at her and then she was slammed into the bookcase. For a while after that, everything was simply chaos.

Books and knickknacks were falling around her. She was trying to get her balance, trying to push the heaviness of a furry body away from her. The wolf was falling back, then jumping again as she twisted sideways to get away.

And the strangest thing was that she actually *was* getting away. Or at least evading the worst of the wolf's lunges, which seemed to be aimed at knocking her to the floor. Her body was moving as if this were somehow instinctive to her, as if she knew how to do this.

But I *don't* know this. I never fight . . . and I've certainly never played dodgeball with a wolf before. . . .

As she thought it, her movements slowed. She didn't feel sure and instinctive any longer. She felt confused.

And the wolf seemed to know it. Its eyes glowed eerily yellow in the light of a lamp that was lying on its side. They were such strange eyes, more intense and more savage than any animal's she'd ever seen. She saw it draw its legs beneath it.

Move—*now*, the mysterious new part of her mind snapped.

Hannah moved. The wolf hit the bookcase with incredible force, and then the bookcase itself was falling. Hannah flung herself sideways in time to avoid being crushed—but the case fell with an unholy noise directly in front of the door.

Trapped, the dark cool voice in Hannah's mind noted analytically. No exit anymore, except the window.

"Hannah? Hannah?" It was Paul's voice just outside the room. The door flew open—all of four inches. It jammed against the fallen bookcase. "God—what's going on in there? Hannah? Hannah!" He sounded panicked now, banging the door uselessly against the blockage.

Don't think about him, the new part of Hannah's mind said sharply, but Hannah couldn't help it. He sounded so desperate. She opened her mouth to shout back to him, her concentration broken.

And the wolf lunged.

This time Hannah didn't move fast enough. A terrible weight smashed into her and she was falling, flying. She landed hard, her head smacking into the floorboards.

It *hurt*.

Even as she felt it, everything grayed out. Her vision went sparkling, her mind soared away from the pain, and a strange thought flickered through her head.

I'm dead now. It's over again. Oh, Isis, Goddess of Life, guide me to the other world. . . .

"Hannah! Hannah! What's going on in there?" Paul's frantic voice came to her dimly.

Hannah's vision cleared and the bizarre thoughts vanished. She wasn't soaring in sparkling emptiness and she wasn't dead. She was lying on the floor with a book's sharp corner in the small of her back and a wolf on her chest.

Even in the midst of her terror, she felt a strange appalled fascination. She had never seen a wild animal this close. She could see the white-tipped guard hairs standing erect on its face and neck; she could see saliva glistening on its lolling red tongue. She could smell its breath—humid and hot, vaguely doglike but much wilder.

And she couldn't move, she realized. The wolf was as long as she was tall, and it weighed more than she did. Pinned underneath it, she was utterly helpless. All she could do was lie there shivering as the narrow, almost delicate muzzle got closer and closer to her face.

Her eyes closed involuntarily as she felt the cold wetness of its nose on her cheek. It wasn't an affectionate gesture. The wolf was nudging at strands of her hair that had fallen across her face. Using its muzzle like a hand to push the hair away.

Oh, God, please make it stop, Hannah thought. But she was the only one who could stop this—and she didn't know how.

Now the cold nose was moving across her cheekbone. Its sniffing was loud in her ear. The wolf seemed to be smelling her, tasting her, and looking at her all at once.

No. Not looking at *me*. Looking at my birthmark.

It was another one of those ridiculous, impossible thoughts—and it snapped into place like the last piece in a puzzle deep inside her. Irrational as it was, Hannah felt absolutely certain it was true. And it set off the cool wind voice in her mind again.

Reach out, the voice whispered, quiet and businesslike. Feel around you. The weapon has to be there somewhere. You saw it on the bookcase. *Find* it.

The wolf stopped its explorations, seeming satisfied. It lifted its head . . . and laughed.

Really laughed. It was the eeriest and most frightening thing Hannah had ever seen. The big mouth opened, panting, showing teeth, and the yellow eyes blazed with hot bestial triumph.

Hurry, hurry.

Hannah's eyes were helplessly fixed on the sharp white teeth ten inches away from her face, but her hand was creeping out, feeling along the smooth pine floorboards around her. Her fingers glided over books, over the feathery texture of a fern—and then over something square and cold and faced with glass.

The wolf didn't seem to notice. Its lips were pulling back farther and farther. Not laughing anymore. Hannah could see its short front teeth and its long curving canines. She could see its forehead wrinkling. And she could *feel* its body vibrate in a low and vicious growl.

The sound of absolute savagery.

The cool wind voice had taken over Hannah's mind completely. It was telling her what would happen next. The wolf would sink his teeth into her throat and then shake her, tearing skin and ripping muscles away. Her blood would spray like a fountain. It would fill her severed windpipe and her lungs and her mouth. She would die gasping and choking, maybe drowning before she bled out.

Except . . . that she had silver in her hand. A silver picture frame.

Kill it, the cool voice whispered. You've got the right weapon. Hit it dead in the eye with a corner. Drive silver into its brain.

Hannah's ordinary mind didn't even try to figure out how a picture frame could possibly be the right weapon. It didn't object, either. But faint and faraway, there came another voice in her head. Like the cool wind voice, it wasn't hers, but it wasn't someone else's, either. It was a clear crystal voice that seemed to sparkle in jeweled colors as it spoke.

You are not a killer. You don't kill. You have never killed, no matter what happened to you. *You do not kill.*

I don't kill, Hannah thought slowly, in agreement.

Then you're going to *die,* the cool wind voice said brutally, much louder than the crystal voice. Because this animal won't stop until either it's dead or you are. There's no other way to deal with these creatures.

Then it happened. The wolf's mouth opened. In a lightning-fast move, it darted for her throat.

Hannah didn't think. She brought the picture frame up . . . and slammed it into the side of the wolf's head.

Not into the eye. Into the ear.

She felt the impact—hard metal against sensitive flesh. The wolf gave a yelping squeal and staggered sideways, shaking its head and hitting at its face with a forepaw. Its weight was off her for an instant and an instant was all Hannah needed.

Her body moved without her conscious direction, sliding out from under the wolf, twisting and jumping to her feet.

She kept her grasp on the picture frame.

Now. Look around! The bookcase—no, you can't move it. The window! Go for the window.

But the wolf had stopped shaking its head. Even as Hannah started across the room, it turned and saw her. In one flowing, bushy leap it put itself between her and the window. Then it stood looking at her, every hair on its body bristling. Its teeth were bared, its ears upright, and its eyes glared with pure hatred and menace.

It's going to spring, Hannah realized.

I am not a killer. I can't kill.

You don't have any choice—

The wolf sprang.

But it never reached her. Something else came soaring through the window and knocked it off course.

This time, Hannah's eyes and brain identified the creature at once. Another wolf. My *God*, what is going on?

The new animal was gray-brown, smaller than the black wolf and not as striking. Its legs were amazingly delicate, twined with veins and sinews like a racehorse's.

A female, something faraway in Hannah's mind said with dreamlike certainty.

Both wolves had recovered their balance now. They were

on their feet bristling. The room smelled like a zoo.

And now I'm really going to die, Hannah thought. I'm going to be torn to pieces by *two* wolves. She was still clutching the picture frame, but she knew there was no chance of fighting them both off at once. They were going to rip her to bits, quarreling over who got more of her.

Her heart was pounding so hard that it shook her body, and her ears were ringing. The female wolf was staring at her with eyes more amber than yellow, and Hannah stared back, mesmerized, waiting for it to make its move.

The wolf held the gaze for another moment, as if studying Hannah's face—in particular the left side of her face. Her cheek. Then she turned her back to Hannah and faced the black wolf.

And snarled.

Protecting me, Hannah thought, stunned. It was unbelievable—but she was beyond disbelief at this point. She had stepped out of her ordinary life and into a fairy tale full of almost-human wolves. The entire world had gone crazy and all she could do was try to deal with each moment as it came.

They're going to fight, the cool wind voice in her mind told her. As soon as they're into it, run for the window.

At that moment everything erupted into bedlam. The gray wolf had launched herself at the black. The room echoed with the sound of snarling—and of teeth clicking together as both wolves snapped again and again.

Hannah couldn't make out what was going on in the fight. It was just a blurred chaos as the wolves circled and darted and leaped and ducked. But it was by far the most terrifying thing she had ever witnessed. Like the worst dog fight imaginable, like the feeding frenzy of sharks. Both animals seemed to have gone berserk.

Suddenly there was a yelp of pain. Blood welled up on the gray female's flank.

She's too small, Hannah thought. Too light. She doesn't have a chance.

Help her, the crystal voice whispered.

It was an insane suggestion. Hannah couldn't even imagine trying to get in the middle of that snarling whirlwind. But somehow she found herself moving anyway. Placing herself behind the gray wolf. It didn't matter that she didn't believe she was doing it, or that she had no idea how to team up with a wolf in fighting another wolf. She was there and she was holding her silver picture frame high.

The black wolf pulled away from the fight to stare at her.

And there they stood, all three of them panting, Hannah with fear and the wolves with exertion. They were frozen like a tableau in the middle of the wrecked office, all looking at each other tensely. The black wolf on one side, his eyes shining with single-minded menace. The gray wolf on the other, blood matting her coat, bits of fur floating away from her. And Hannah right behind her, holding up the picture frame in a shaking hand.

Hannah's ears were filled with the deep reverberating sound of growling.

And then a deafening report that cut through the room like a knife.

A gunshot.

The black wolf yelped and staggered.

Hannah's senses had been focused on what was going on inside the room for so long that it was a shock to realize there was anything *outside* it. She was dimly aware that Paul's yells had stopped some time ago, but she hadn't stopped to consider what that meant.

Now, with adrenaline washing over her, she heard his voice.

"Hannah! Get out of the way!"

The shout was tense, edged with fear and anger—and determination. It came from the opposite side of the room, from the darkness outside the window.

Paul was there at the broken window with a gun. His face was pale and his hand was shaking. He was aiming in the general direction of the wolves. If he fired again he might hit either of them.

"Get into a corner!" The gun bobbed nervously.

Hannah heard herself say, "Don't shoot!"

Her voice came out hoarse and unused-sounding. She moved to get in between the gun and the wolves.

"Don't shoot," she said again. "Don't hit the gray one."

"Hit the gray one?" Paul's voice rose in something like hysterical laughter. "I don't even know if I can hit the wall! This is the first time I've ever shot a gun. So just—just try to get out of the way!"

"No!" Hannah moved toward him, holding out her hand. "I can shoot. Just give it to me—"

"Just move out of the *way*—"

The gun went off.

For an instant Hannah couldn't see where the bullet had gone and she wondered wildly if *she* had been shot. Then she saw that the black wolf was lurching backward. Blood dripped from its neck.

Steel won't kill it, the wind voice hissed. You're only making it more angry. . . .

But the black wolf was swinging its head to look with blazing eyes from Hannah with her picture frame to Paul with his gun, to the gray wolf with her teeth. The gray wolf snarled just then and Hannah had never seen an animal look closer to being smug.

"One more shot . . ." Paul breathed. "While it's cornered . . ."

Ears flat, the black wolf turned toward the only other window in the room. It launched into a vaulting leap straight toward the unbroken glass. There was a shattering crash as it went through. Glass fragments flew everywhere, tinkling.

Hannah stared dizzily at the curtains swirling first outside, then inside the room, and then her head snapped around to look at the gray wolf.

Amber eyes met hers directly. It was such a human stare . . . and definitely the look of an equal. Almost the look of a friend.

Then the gray wolf twisted and loped for the newly broken window. Two steps and a leap—she was through.

From somewhere outside there came a long drawn-out howl of anger and defiance. It was fading, as if the wolf was moving away.

Then silence.

Hannah shut her eyes.

Her knees literally felt as if they wanted to buckle. But she made herself move to the window, glass grating under her boots as she stared into the night.

The moon was bright, one day past full. She thought she could just see a dark shape loping toward the open prairie, but it might have been her imagination.

She let out her breath and sagged against the window. The silver picture frame fell to the floor.

"Are you hurt? Are you okay?" Paul was climbing through the other window. He tripped on a wastebasket getting across the room, then he was beside her, grabbing for her shoulders, trying to look her over.

"I think I'm all right." She was numb, was what she was. She felt dazed and fragmented.

He blinked at her. "Um . . . you have some particular fondness for gray wolves or something?"

Hannah shook her head. How could she ever explain?

They stared at each other for a moment, and then, simultaneously, they both sank to the floor, squatting among the shards of glass, breathing hard.

Paul's face was white, his red hair disheveled, his eyes large and stunned. He ran a shaky hand over his forehead, then put the gun down and patted it. He twisted his neck to stare at the wreck of his office, the overturned bookcase, the scattered books and knickknacks, the two broken windows, the glass fragments, the bullet hole, the flecks of blood, and the tufts of wolf hair that still drifted across the pine floorboards.

Hannah said faintly, "So who was at the door?"

Paul blinked twice. "Nobody. Nobody was at the door." He added almost dreamily, "I wonder if wolves can ring doorbells?"

"*What?*"

Paul turned to look straight at her.

"Has it ever occurred to you," he blurted, "that you may *not* be paranoid after all? I mean, that something weird and uncanny really *is* out to get you?"

"Very funny," Hannah whispered.

"I mean—" Paul gestured around the room, half-laughing. He looked punch-drunk. "I mean, you *said* something was going to happen—and something did." He stopped laughing and looked at her with wondering speculation. "You really did know, didn't you?"

Hannah glared at the man who was supposed to guide her back to sanity. "Are you *crazy?*"

Paul blinked. He looked shocked and embarrassed, then he glanced away and shook his head. "God, I don't know. Sorry; that wasn't very professional, was it? But . . ." He stared out the window. "Well, for a moment it just seemed possible that you've got some kind of secret locked up there in your brain. Something . . . extraordinary."

Hannah said nothing. She was trying to forget about too many things at once: the new part of her that whispered strategies, the wolves with human eyes, the silver picture frame. She had no idea what all these things added up to, and she didn't want to know. She wanted to force them away from her and go back to the safe, ordinary world of Sacajawea High School.

Paul cleared his throat, still looking out the window. His voice was uncertain and almost apologetic. "It can't be true, of course. There's got to be a rational explanation. But—well, if it were true, it occurs to me that somebody had better unlock that secret. Before something worse happens."

CHAPTER 3

The sleek white limousine raced through the night like a dolphin underwater, carrying Thierry Descouedres away from the airport. It was taking him to his Las Vegas mansion, white walls and palm trees, limpid blue fountains and tiled terraces. Rooms full of artwork and museum-quality furniture. Everything anyone could ask for.

He shut his eyes and leaned back against the crimson cushions, wishing he were somewhere else.

"How was Hawaii, sir?" The driver's voice came from the front seat.

Thierry opened his eyes. Nilsson was a good driver. He seemed to be about Thierry's own age, around nineteen, with a neat ponytail, dark glasses despite the fact that it was night-time, and a discreet expression.

"Wet, Nilsson," Thierry said softly. He stared out the window. "Hawaii was very . . . wet."

"But you didn't find what you were looking for."

"No. I didn't find what I was looking for . . . again."

"I'm sorry, sir."

"Thank you, Nilsson." Thierry tried to look past his own reflection in the window. It was disturbing, seeing that young man with the white-blond hair and the old, old eyes looking back at him. He had such a pensive expression . . . so lost and so sad.

Like somebody always looking for something he can't find, Thierry thought.

He turned away from the window in determination.

"Everything been going all right while I've been gone?" he asked, picking up his cellular phone. Work. Work always helped. Kept you busy, kept your mind off things, kept you away from *yourself*, basically.

"Fine, I think, sir. Mr. James and Miss Poppy are back."

"That's good. They'll make the next Circle Daybreak meeting." Thierry's finger hovered over a button on the phone, considering whom to call. Whose need might be the most urgent.

But before he could touch it, the phone buzzed.

Thierry pressed send and held it to his ear. "Thierry."

"Sir? It's me, Lupe. Can you hear me?" The voice was faint and broken by static, but distant as it was, Thierry could hear that the caller sounded weak.

"Lupe? Are you all right?"

"I got in a fight, sir. I'm a little torn up." She gave a gasping chuckle. "But you should see the *other* wolf."

Thierry reached for a leather-bound address book and a gold Mont Blanc pen. "That's not funny, Lupe. You shouldn't be fighting."

"I know, sir, but—"

"You've really got to restrain yourself."

"Yes, sir, but—"

"Tell me where you are, and I'll have somebody pick you up. Get you to a doctor." Thierry made a practice mark with the pen. No ink came out. He stared at the nib of it in mild disbelief. "You buy an eight-hundred-dollar pen and then it doesn't write," he murmured.

"Sir, you're not listening to me. You don't understand. *I've found her.*"

Thierry stopped trying to make the pen write. He stared at it, at his own long fingers holding the chunky, textured gold barrel, knowing that this sight would be impressed on his memory as if burned in with a torch.

"Did you hear me, sir? I've found her."

When his voice came out at last, it was strangely distant. "Are you sure?"

"Yes. Yes, sir, I'm sure. She's got the mark and everything. Her name is Hannah Snow."

Thierry reached over the front seat and grabbed the astonished Nilsson with a hand like iron. He said very quietly in the driver's ear, "Do you have a pencil?"

"A pencil?"

"Something that writes, Nilsson. An instrument to make marks on paper. Do you *have* one? Quick, because if I lose this connection, you're fired."

"I've got a pen, sir." One-handed, Nilsson fished in his pocket and produced a Bic.

"Your salary just doubled." Thierry took the pen and sat back. "Where are you, Lupe?"

"The Badlands of Montana, sir. Near a town called Medicine Rock. But there's something else, sir." Lupe's voice seemed less steady all of a sudden. "The other wolf that fought me—he saw her, too. And he got away."

Thierry's breath caught. "I see."

"I'm sorry." Lupe was suddenly talking quickly, in a burst of emotion. "Oh, Thierry, I'm sorry. I tried to stop him. But he got away—and now I'm afraid he's off telling . . . *her.*"

"You couldn't help it, Lupe. And I'll be there myself, soon. I'll be there to take care of—everything." Thierry looked at the driver. "We've got to make some stops, Nilsson. First, the Harman store."

"The witch place?"

"Exactly. You can triple your salary if you get there fast."

When Hannah got to Paul Winfield's house the next afternoon, the sheriff was there. Chris Grady was an honest-to-goodness Western sheriff, complete with boots, broad-brimmed hat, and vest. The only thing missing, Hannah thought as she walked around to the back of the house where Paul was hammering boards across the broken windows, was a horse.

"Hi, Chris," she said.

The sheriff nodded, sun-weathered skin crinkling at the corners of her eyes. She took off her hat and ran a hand through shoulder-length auburn hair. "I see you found yourself a couple of giant timber wolves, Hannah. You're not hurt, are you?"

Hannah shook her head no. She tried to summon up a smile but failed. "I think they were maybe wolf-dogs or something. Pure-bred wolves aren't so aggressive."

"That print wasn't made by any wolf-dog," Chris said. On the concrete flagstones outside the window there was a paw print made in blood. It was similar to a dog's footprint, with four pads plus claw marks showing. But it was more than six inches long by just over five inches wide.

"Judging from that, it's the biggest wolf ever heard of around here, bigger than the White Wolf of the Judith." The sheriff's eyes drifted to the empty rectangles of the broken windows. "Big and mean. You people be careful. Something's going on here that I don't like. I'll let you know if we catch your wolves."

She nodded to Paul, who was sucking his finger after banging it with the hammer. Then she set her hat back on her head and strode off to her car.

Hannah stared at the paw print silently. Everyone else thought there was something going on. Everyone but her.

Because there can't be, she thought. Because it *has* to all be in my head. It has to be something I can figure out and fix quick . . . something I can control.

"Thanks for seeing me again so soon," she said to Paul.

"Oh . . ." He gestured, tucking the hammer under his arm. "It's no trouble. I want to get to the bottom of what's upsetting you as much as you do. And," he admitted under his breath as he let them in the house, "I don't actually have any other patients."

Hannah followed him down a hallway and into his office. It was dim inside, the boards across the windows reducing the late afternoon sunlight to separate oddly-angled shafts.

She sat in the contoured chair. "The only thing is, how *can* we get to the bottom of it? I don't understand what's upsetting me, either. It's all too strange. I mean, on the one hand, I'm clearly insane." She spoke flatly as Paul took his seat on the opposite side of the desk. "I have crazy dreams, I think the world is going to end, I have the feeling I'm being followed, and yesterday I started hearing voices in my head. On the other hand, me being insane doesn't explain wolves jumping through the windows."

"Voices?" Paul murmured, looking around for a pencil. Then he gave up and faced her. "Yeah, I know. I understand the temptation. Last night after having those wolves stare at me, I was about ready to believe that there had to be something . . ." He trailed off and shook his head, lifting papers on his desk to glance under them. "Something . . . really strange going on. But now it's daytime, and we're all rational people, and we realize that we have to deal with things rationally. And, actually, you know, I think I may have come up with a rational explanation." He found a pencil and with an expression of vast relief began to waggle it between his fingers.

Hope stirred inside Hannah. "An explanation?"

"Yeah. I mean, first of all, it's possible that your premonitions and things are entirely unconnected with the wolves. People never want to believe in coincidence, but it happens. But even if the two things are connected—well, I don't think that means that anybody's after you. It could be that there's some sort of disturbance in this area—something that's stirring up the whole ecosystem, making wolves crazy, doing who knows what to other animals . . . and that you're somehow sensing this. You're *attuned* to it somehow. Maybe it's earthquake weather or—or sunspots or negative ions in the air. But whatever it is, it's causing you to think that some terrible disaster is coming. That the world is ending or that you're about to be killed."

Hannah felt the hope sink inside her, and it was more painful than not having had it at all. "I suppose that could happen," she said. She didn't want to hurt his feelings. "But how does it explain this?"

She reached into the canvas bag she carried instead of a purse and pulled out a folded slip of paper.

Paul took the paper and read it. "'They've seen you. They're going to tell him. This is your last chance to get away.'" He stuck the pencil in his mouth. "Hmmm . . ."

"I found it this morning wrapped around my toothbrush," Hannah said quietly.

"And it's your handwriting?"

She shut her eyes and nodded.

"And you don't remember writing it."

"I *didn't* write it. I know I didn't." She opened her eyes and took a deep breath. "The notes scare me. Everything that's happening scares me. I don't understand any of it, and I don't see how I'm supposed to *fix* it if I don't understand it."

Paul considered, chewing on the pencil gently. "Look— whatever's happening, whoever's writing the notes, I think your subconscious mind is trying to tell you something. The dreams are evidence of that. But it's not telling you enough. There's something I was going to suggest, something I don't exactly believe in, but that we can try anyway. Something to get to your subconscious directly so we can ask it what's going on."

Get to her subconscious directly. . . . Hannah held her breath. "Hypnosis?"

Paul nodded. "I'm not a big hypnosis fan. It's not some magical trance like TV and the movies want you to believe. It's just a state of mind where you're a little more relaxed, a little more likely to be able to remember threatening things without choking up. But it's nothing you can't achieve yourself by doing breathing exercises at home."

Hannah wasn't happy. Hypnosis still seemed to mean giving up control. If not to Paul, then to her own subconscious.

But what else am I supposed to do? She sat and listened to the quiet helplessness in her mind for a moment. Not a peep from the cool wind voice or the crystal voice—and that was *good,* as far as she was concerned. Still, it pointed up the fact that she didn't have an alternative.

She looked at Paul. "Okay. Let's do it."

"Great." He stood, then reached for a book on the corner of his desk. "Always assuming I remember how. . . . Okay, why don't you lie down on the couch?"

Hannah hesitated, then shrugged. If I'm going to do it, I might as well do it right. She lay down and stared at the dark beams in the ceiling. In spite of how miserable she was feeling, she had an almost irresistible impulse to giggle.

Here she was on a real psychologist's couch, waiting to be hypnotized. Her friends at school would never consider even going to a shrink—out here in Montana craziness was okay. After all, you had to be a little eccentric to be living in this hard land in the first place. What wasn't okay was admitting you couldn't deal with it on your own, paying too much attention to it, asking for help. And allowing yourself to be hypnotized was even worse.

They all think I'm the most independent and together of any of them. If they could see me now.

"Okay, I want you to get comfortable and shut your eyes," Paul said. He was perched with one hip on the edge of his desk, leg swinging, book in hand. His voice was quiet and soothing—the professional voice.

Hannah shut her eyes.

"Now I want you to imagine yourself floating. Just floating and feeling very relaxed. There's nothing you need to think about and nowhere you need to go. And now you're seeing yourself enveloped by a beautiful violet light. It's bathing your entire body and it's making you more and more relaxed . . ."

The couch *was* surprisingly comfortable. Its curves fit under her, supporting her without being intrusive. It was easy to imagine that she was floating, easy to imagine the light around her.

"And now you feel yourself floating down deeper . . . into a deeper state of relaxation . . . and you're surrounded by a deep blue light. The blue light is all around you, shining through you, and it's making you more comfortable, more relaxed . . ."

The soft soothing voice went on, and at its direction Hannah imagined waves of colored light bathing her body. Deep blue, emerald green, golden yellow, glowing orange. Hannah saw it all. It was amazing and effortless; her mind just showed her the pictures.

And as the colors came and went she felt herself becoming more and more relaxed, warm and almost weightless. She couldn't feel the couch underneath her any longer. She was floating on light.

"And now you're seeing a ruby red light, very deep, very relaxing. You're so relaxed; you're calm and comfortable, and everything feels safe. Nothing will upset you; you can answer all my questions without ever feeling distressed. Do you understand me?"

"Yes," Hannah said. She was aware of saying it, but it wasn't exactly as if *she* had said it. She wasn't aware of *planning* to say it. Something within her seemed to be answering Paul using her voice.

But it wasn't frightening. She still felt relaxed, floating in the ruby light.

"All right. I'm now speaking to Hannah's subconscious. You will be able to remember things that Hannah's waking mind isn't aware of—even things that have been repressed. Do you understand?"

"Yes." Again, the voice seemed to come before Hannah decided to speak.

"Good. Now, I've got this last note here, the one you found wrapped around your toothbrush this morning. Do you remember this note?"

"Yes." Of course.

"Okay, that's good. And now I want you to go back in your mind, back to the time that this note was written."

This time Hannah was aware of a need to speak. "But

how can I do that? I don't *know* when it was written. I didn't write—"

"Just—just—just let go, Hannah," Paul said, overriding her. His voice soothing again, he added, "Feel relaxed, feel yourself becoming very relaxed, and let your conscious mind go. Just tell yourself to go back to the time this note was written. Don't worry about *how*. See the ruby light and think 'I will go back.' Are you doing that?"

"Yes," Hannah said. Go back, she told herself gamely. Just relax and go back, okay?

"And now, a picture is beginning to form in your mind. You are seeing something. What are you seeing?"

Hannah felt something inside her give way. She seemed to be falling into the ruby light. Her ordinary mind was suspended; it seemed to have been shuttled off to the side somewhere. In this odd dreamlike state, nothing could surprise her.

Paul's voice was gently insistent. "What are you seeing?"

Hannah saw it.

A tiny picture that seemed to open up, unfold as she stared at it.

"I see myself," she whispered.

"Where are you?"

"I don't know. Wait, maybe I'm in my room." She could see herself, wearing something long and white—a nightgown. No, she *was* that self, she was in her bedroom, wearing her nightgown. She was in Paul's office, lying on the couch, but she was in her bedroom at the same time. How strange, she thought dimly.

"All right, now the picture will get clearer. You'll begin to see things around you. Just relax and you'll begin to see them. Now, what are you doing?"

Without feeling anything—except a kind of distant amusement and resignation—Hannah said, "Writing a note."

Paul muttered something that sounded like, *"Aha."* But it might have been, "Uh-*huh*." Then he said softly, "And why are you writing it?"

"I don't know—to warn myself. I have to warn myself."

"About what?"

Hannah felt herself shake her own head helplessly.

"Okay . . . what are you feeling as you write it?"

"Oh . . ." That was easy. Paul was undoubtedly expecting her to say something like "fear" or "anxiety." But that wasn't the strongest thing she was feeling. Not the strongest at all.

"Longing," Hannah whispered. She moved her head restlessly on the couch. "Just—longing."

"I beg your pardon?"

"I want—so much . . . I want . . ."

"What do you want?"

"Him." It came out as a sob. Hannah's ordinary mind watched somewhere in amazement, but Hannah's body was entirely taken over by the feeling, racked with it. "I know it's impossible. It's danger and death to me. But *I don't care.* I can't help it . . ."

"Whoa, whoa, whoa. I mean, you're feeling very relaxed. You're very calm and you can answer my questions. Who is this person that you're longing for?"

"The one who comes," Hannah said softly and hopelessly. "He's wicked and evil . . . I know that. She explained it all to me. And I know he'll kill me. The way he always has. *But I want him.*"

She was trembling. She could feel her own body radiating heat—and she could hear Paul swallow. Somehow in this expanded state of consciousness she seemed to be able to see him, as if she could be everywhere at once. She knew he was sitting there on the edge of the desk, looking at her dazedly, bewildered by the transformation in the young woman on his couch.

She knew he could see *her*, her face pale and glowing from inner heat, her breath coming quickly, her body gripped by a fine muscular tremor. And she knew he was stirred—and frightened.

"Oh, boy." Paul's breath came out and he shifted on the desk. He bowed his head, then lifted it, looking for a pencil. "Okay, I have to admit, I'm lost. Let's just go back to the beginning here. You feel that somebody is after you, and that he's tried to kill you before? Some old boyfriend who's stalking you, maybe?"

"No. He hasn't tried to kill me. He *has* killed me."

"He has killed you." Paul bit his pencil. He muttered, "I should have known better than to have started this. I don't believe in hypnosis anyway."

"And he's going to do it again. I'll die before my seventeenth birthday. It's my punishment for loving him. It always happens that way."

"Right. Okay. Okay, let's try something *really* basic here. . . . Does this mystery guy have a name?"

Hannah lifted a hand and let it drop. "When?" she whispered.

"What?"

"When?"

"When what? What?" Paul shook his head. "Oh, hell—"

Hannah spoke precisely. "He's used different names at different times. He's had—hundreds, I guess. But I think of him as Thierry. Thierry Descouedres. Because that's the one he's used for the last couple of lifetimes."

There was a long silence. Then Paul said, "The last couple of . . . ?"

"Lifetimes. It may still be his name now. The last time I saw him he said he wouldn't bother to change it anymore. He wouldn't bother to hide any longer."

Paul said, "Oh, God." He stood, walked to the window, and put his head in his hands. Then he turned back to Hannah. "Are we talking about . . . I mean, tell me we're not talking about . . ." He paused and then his voice came out soft and boneless. "The Big R? You know . . ." He winced. "Reincarnation?"

A long silence.

Then Hannah heard her own voice say flatly, "He hasn't been reincarnated."

"Oh." Paul's breath came out in relief. "Well, thank God. You had me scared there for a minute."

"He's been alive all this time," Hannah said. "He isn't human, you know."

CHAPTER 4

Thierry knelt by the window, careful not to make a noise or disturb the dry earth beneath him. It was a skill so familiar to his body that he might have been born with it. Darkness was his native environment; he could melt into a shadow at an instant's notice or move more quietly than a stalking cat. But right now he was looking into the light.

He could see her. Just the curve of her shoulder and the spill of her hair, but he knew it was her.

Beside him, Lupe was crouched, her thin body human but quivering with animal alertness and tension. She whispered, softer than a breath, "All right?"

Thierry tore his gaze from that shoulder to look at her. Lupe's face was bruised, one eye almost closed, lower lip torn. But she was smiling. She'd stuck around Medicine Rock until Thierry had arrived, tailing the girl called Hannah Snow, making sure no harm came to her.

Thierry took Lupe's hand and kissed it. *You're an angel,* he told her, and made even less sound than she had in speaking because he didn't use his vocal cords at all. His voice was telepathic. *And you deserve a long vacation. My limo's at the tourist resort in Clearwater; take it to the airport at Billings.*

"But—you're not planning to stay here alone, are you? You need backup, sir. If *she* comes—"

I can take care of things. I brought something to protect Hannah. Besides, she won't do anything until she talks to me.

"But—"

Lupe, go. His tone was gentle, but it was unmistakably not the urging of a friend anymore. It was the order of her liege lord, Thierry of the Night World, who was accustomed to being obeyed. Funny, Thierry thought, how you never realized *how* accustomed you were to being obeyed until somebody defied you. Now he turned away from Lupe and looked through the cracks in the boarded-up window again.

And promptly forgot that Lupe existed. The girl on the couch had turned. He could see her face.

Shock coursed through him.

He had known it was her—but he hadn't known that it would *look* so much like her. Like the way she had looked the first time, the first time she had been born, the first time he had seen her. This was what he thought of as her true face, and though he'd seen various approximations of it through the years, he'd never seen *it* again. Until now.

This was the exact image of the girl he'd fallen in love with.

The same long, straight fair hair, like silk in different shades of wheat color, spilling over her shoulders. The same wide gray eyes that seemed full of light. The same steady expression, the same tender mouth, upper lip indenting the lower to give her a look of unintentional sensuality. The same fine bone structure, the high cheekbones and graceful line of jaw that made her a sculptor's dream.

The only thing that was different was the birthmark.

The psychic brand.

It was the color of watered wine held up to the light, of watermelon ice, of a pink tourmaline, the palest of gemstones. Blushing rose. Like one large petal, slantwise beneath her cheekbone. As if she'd laid a rose against her cheek for a moment and it had left its imprint on her flesh.

To Thierry, it was beautiful, because it was part of her. She'd worn it in every lifetime after the first. But at the same time the very sight of it made his throat clamp shut and his fists clench in helpless grief and fury—fury against himself. The mark was *his* shame, his punishment. And his penance was to watch her wear it in her innocence through the years.

He would pour out his blood on the dry Montana dirt right now if it would take the mark away. But nothing in either the Night World or the human world could do that—at least nothing he'd found in uncounted years of searching.

Oh, Goddess, he loved her.

He hadn't allowed himself to *feel* it for so long—because the feeling could drive him insane while he was away from her. But now it came over him in a flood that he couldn't have resisted if he'd tried. It made his heart pound and his body tremble. The sight of her lying there, warm and alive, separated from him by only a few flimsy boards and an equally flimsy human male . . .

He wanted her. He wanted to yank off the boards, step through the window, brush aside the red-haired man, and take her in his arms. He wanted to carry her off into the night, holding her close to his heart, to some secret place where nobody could ever find her to hurt her.

He didn't. He knew . . . from experience . . . that it didn't work. He'd done it once or twice, and he'd paid for it. She had hated him before she died.

He would never risk that again.

And so now, on this spring night near the turn of the millennium in the state of Montana in the United States of America, all Thierry could do was kneel outside a window and watch the newest incarnation of his only love.

He didn't realize at first, though, what his only love was actually doing. Lupe had told him that Hannah Snow was seeing a psychologist. But it was only now, listening to what was going on in the room that Thierry slowly realized exactly what Hannah and the psychologist were up to.

They were trying to recover her memories. Using hypnosis. Breaking into her subconscious as if it were some bank vault.

It was dangerous.

Not just because the guy performing the hypnosis didn't seem to know what he was doing. But because Hannah's memory was a time-bomb, full of trauma for her and deadly knowledge for any human.

They shouldn't be doing this.

Every muscle in Thierry's body was tense. But there was no way he could stop it. He could only listen—and wait.

Paul repeated with slow resignation, "He's not human."

"No. He's a Lord of the Night World. He's powerful . . . and evil," Hannah whispered. "He's lived for thousands of years." She added, almost absently, "*I'm* the one who's been reincarnated."

"Oh, terrific. Well, that's a twist."

"You don't believe me?"

Paul seemed to suddenly remember that he was talking with a patient—and a hypnotized patient at that. "No, I—I mean, I don't know what to believe. If it's a fantasy, there's got to be something underneath it, some psychological reason for you to make it all up. And that's what we're looking for. What all this means to *you*." He hesitated, then said with new determination, "Let's take you back to the first time you met this guy. Okay, I want you to relax in the light; you're feeling very good. And now I want you to go back through time, just like turning back the pages of a book. In your mind, go back. . . ."

Hannah's ordinary mind was intruding, waking up, overriding the dreamy part of her that had been answering Paul's questions. "Wait, I—I don't know if that's a good idea."

"We can't figure this out until we find out what it all symbolizes; what it means to you."

Hannah still didn't feel convinced, but she had the feeling she wasn't supposed to argue under hypnosis. Maybe it doesn't matter, though, she thought. I'm waking up now; I probably won't be *able* to go back.

"I want you to see yourself as fifteen years old, see yourself as fifteen. Go back to the time when you were fifteen. And now I want you to see yourself at twelve years old; go in your mind to the time when you are twelve. Now go farther back, see yourself at nine years old, at six years old, at three years old. Now go back and see yourself as a baby, as an infant. Feel very comfortable and see yourself as a tiny baby."

Hannah couldn't help but listen. She *did* feel comfortable, and her mind did show her pictures as the years seemed to turn back. It was like watching a film of her life running backward, herself getting smaller and smaller, and in the end tiny and bald.

"And now," the soothing, irresistible voice said, "I want you to go *farther* back. Back to the time before you were born. The time before you were born as Hannah Snow. You are floating in the red light, you feel very relaxed, and you are going back, back . . . to the time when you *first* met this man you think of as Thierry. Whatever that time might be, go back. Go back to the first time."

Hannah was being drawn down a tunnel.

She had no control and she was scared. It wasn't like the rumored near-death tunnel. It was red, with translucent, shining, pulsing walls—something like a womb. And she was being pulled or sucked through it at ever-increasing speed.

No, she thought. But she couldn't say anything. It was all happening too fast and she couldn't make a sound.

"Back to the first time," Paul intoned, and his words set up a sort of echo in Hannah's head, a whispering of many voices. As if a hundred Hannahs had all gotten together and murmured sibilantly, "The First Time. The First Time."

"Go back . . . and you will begin to see pictures. You will see yourself, maybe in a strange place. Go back and see this."

The First Time . . .

No, Hannah thought again. And something very deep inside her whimpered, "I don't want to see it." But she was still being pulled through the soft red tunnel, faster and faster. She had a feeling of unimaginable distance being crossed. And then . . . she had a feeling of some threshold being reached.

The First Time.

She exploded into darkness, squirted out of the tunnel like a watermelon seed between wet fingers.

Silence. Dark. And then—a picture. It opened like a tiny leaf unfolding out of a seed, got bigger until it surrounded her. It was like a scene from a movie, except that it was all around her, she seemed to be floating in the middle of it.

"What do you see?" came Paul's voice softly from very far away.

"I see . . . me," Hannah said. "It's me—it looks just like me. Except that I don't have a birthmark." She was full of wonder.

"Where are you? What do you see yourself doing?"

"I don't know where I am." Hannah was too amazed to be frightened now. It was so strange . . . she could see this better than any memory of her real life. The scene was incredibly detailed. At the same time, it was completely unfamiliar to her. "What I'm doing . . . I'm holding . . . something. A rock. And I'm doing something with it to a little tiny . . . something." She sighed, defeated, then added, "I'm wearing *animal skins*! It's a sort of shirt and pants all made of skins. It's unbelievably . . . primitive. Paul, there's a cave behind me."

"Sounds like you're *really* far back." Paul's voice sounded in stark contrast to Hannah's wonder and excitement. He was clearly bored. Amused, resigned, but bored.

"And—there's a girl beside me and she looks like Chess. Like my best friend, Chess. She's got the same face, the same eyes. She's wearing skins, too . . . some kind of skin dress."

"Yeah, and it has about the detail of most of the past-life regressions in this book," Paul said wryly. Hannah could tell he was flipping pages. "You're doing *something* to *something* with a rock. You're wearing *some kind* of skins. The book's full of descriptions like that. People who want to imagine themselves in the olden days, but who don't know the first thing about them," he muttered to himself.

Hannah didn't wait for him to remember that he was talking to a hypnotized patient. "But you didn't tell me to *be* the person back then. You just told me to see it."

"Huh? Oh. Okay, then, *be* that person." He said it so casually.

Panic spurted through Hannah. "Wait—I . . ."

But it was happening. She was falling, dissolving, merging into the scene around her. She was becoming the girl in front of the cave.

The First Time . . .

Distantly, she heard her own voice whispering, "I'm holding a flint burin, a tool for drilling. I'm boring holes in the tooth of an arctic fox."

"Be that person," Paul was repeating mechanically, still in the bored voice. Then he said, "What?"

"Mother's going to be furious—I'm supposed to be sorting fruit we stored last winter for the Spring Gathering. There's not much left and it's mostly rotten. But Ran killed a fox and gave the skull to Ket, and we've spent all morning knocking the teeth out and making them into a necklace for Ket. Ket just *has* to have something new to wear every festival."

She heard Paul say softly, "Oh, my God . . ." Then he swallowed and said, "Wait—you want to be a paleontologist, right? You know about old things . . ."

"I want to be a what? I'm going to be a shaman, like Old

Mother. I should get married, but there's nobody I want. Ket keeps telling me I'll meet somebody at a gathering, but I don't think so." She shivered. "Weird—I've got chills all of a sudden. Old Mother says she can't see my destiny. She pretends that's nothing to worry about, but I know *she's* worried. That's why she wants me to be a shaman, so I can fight back if the spirits have something rotten in mind for me."

Paul said, "Hannah—uh, let's just make sure we can get you out of this, all right? You know, in case that should become necessary. Now, when I clap my hands you're going to awaken completely refreshed. Okay? Okay?"

"My name's Hana." It was pronounced slightly differently: *Hah-na.* "And I'm already awake. Ket is laughing at me. She's threading the teeth on a sinew string. She says I'm daydreaming. She's right; I wrecked the hole for this tooth."

"When I clap my hands, you're going to wake up. When I clap my hands, you're going to wake up. You will be Hannah Snow in Montana." A clap. "Hannah, how do you feel?" Another clap. "Hannah? Hannah?"

"It's Hana. Hana of the River People. And I don't know what you're talking about; I can't *be* somebody else." She stiffened. "Wait—something's happening. There's some kind of commotion from the river. Something's going on."

The voice was desperate. "When I clap my hands—"

"*Shh.* Be quiet." Something was happening and she had to see it, she had to know. She had to stand up. . . .

• • •

Hana of the Three Rivers stood up.

"Everybody's all excited by the river," she told Ket.

"Maybe Ran fell in," Ket said. "No, that's too much to hope for. Hana, what am I going to do? He wants to mate me, but I just can't picture it. I want somebody *interesting*, somebody *different*. . . ." She held up the half-finished necklace. "So what do you think?"

Hana barely glanced at her. Ket looked wonderful, with her short dark hair, her glowing slanted green eyes, and her mysterious smile. The necklace was attractive; red beads alternated with delicate milky-white teeth. "Fine, beautiful. You'll break every heart at the gathering. I'm going down to the river."

Ket put down the necklace. "Well, if you insist—wait for me."

The river was broad and fast-flowing, covered with little white-capped waves because it had just been joined by two tributaries. Hana's people had lived in the limestone caves by the three rivers for longer than anyone could remember.

Ket was behind her as Hana made her way through new green cattails to the bend in the river. And then she saw what the fuss was about.

There was a stranger crouching in the reeds. That was exciting enough—strangers didn't come very often. But this stranger was like no man Hana had ever seen.

"It's a demon," Ket whispered, awed.

It was a young man—a boy a few years older than Hana herself. He might have been handsome in other circumstances. His hair was very light blond, lighter than the dry grass of the steppes. His face was well-made; his tall body was lithe. Hana could see almost all of that body because he was only wearing a brief leather loincloth. That didn't bother her; everybody went naked in the summer when it was hot enough. But this wasn't summer; it was spring and the days could still be chilly. No sane person would go traveling without clothes.

But that wasn't what shocked Hana, what held her standing there rigid with her heart pounding so hard she couldn't breathe. It was the rest of the boy's appearance. Ket was right— he was clearly a demon.

His eyes were wrong. More like the eyes of a lynx or a wolverine than the eyes of a person. They seemed to throw the pale sunlight back at you when you looked into them. But the eyes were nothing compared to the teeth. His canine teeth were long and delicately curved. They came to a sharp and very nonhuman point.

Almost involuntarily, Hana looked down at the fox tooth she still held in her palm. Yes, they were like that, only bigger.

The boy was filthy, caked with mud from the river, his blond hair ruffled crazily, his eyes staring wildly from side to side. There was blood on his mouth and chin.

"He's a demon, all right," one of the men said. Five men were standing around the crouching boy, several of them with spears, others with hastily grabbed rocks. "What else could have a human body with animal eyes and teeth?"

"A spirit?" Hana said. She didn't realize that she was going to say it until the words were out. But then, with everybody looking at her, she drew herself up tall. "Whether he's a demon or a spirit, you'd better not hurt him. It's Old Mother who should decide what to do with him. This is a matter for shamans."

"You're not a shaman yet," another of the men said. It was Arno, a very broad-shouldered man who was the leader of the hunters. Hana didn't like him.

And she wasn't sure why she had spoken up in favor of the stranger. There was something in his eyes, the look of a suffering animal. He seemed so alone, and so frightened—and so much in pain, even though there were no visible wounds on his body.

"She's right, we'd better take him to Old Mother," one of the hunters said. "Should we hit him on the head and tie him up, or do you think we can just herd him?"

But at that moment, a high thin sound came to Hana over the rushing of the river. It was a woman screaming.

"Help me! Somebody come help me! Ryl's been attacked!"

CHAPTER 5

Hana turned and hurried up the riverbank. The woman screaming was Sada, her mother's sister, and the girl who was stumbling beside her was Ryl, Hana's little cousin.

Ryl was a pretty girl ten years old. But right now she looked dazed and almost unconscious. And her neck and the front of her leather tunic were smeared with blood.

"What happened?" Hana gasped, running to put her arms around her cousin.

"She was out looking for new greens. I found her lying on the ground—I thought she was dead!" Sada's face contorted in grief. She was speaking rapidly, almost incoherently. "And look at this—look at her neck!"

On Ryl's pale neck, in the center of the blood, Hana could just make out two small marks. They looked like the marks of sharp teeth—but only two teeth.

"It had to be an animal," Ket breathed from behind Hana. "But what animal only leaves the marks of two teeth?"

Hana's heart felt tight and oddly heavy at once—like a stone falling inside her. Sada was already speaking.

"It wasn't an animal! She says it was a man, a boy! She says he threw her down and bit her—and he drank her blood." Sada began to sob, clutching Ryl to her. "Why would he want to do that? Oh, please, somebody help me! My daughter's been hurt!"

Ryl just stared dazedly over her mother's arm.

Ket said faintly, "A boy . . ."

Hana gulped and said, "Let's take her to Old Mother . . ." But then she stopped and looked toward the river.

The men were driving the stranger up the bank. He was snarling, terrified and angry—but when he saw Ryl, his expression changed.

He stared at her, his wounded animal eyes sick and dismayed. To Hana, it seemed as if he could hardly stand to look at her, but he couldn't look away. His gaze was fixed on the little girl's throat.

And then he turned away, his eyes shut, his head falling into his hands. Every movement showed anguish. It was as if all the fight had gone out of him at once.

Hana looked back and forth in horror from the girl with blood on her throat to the stranger with blood on his mouth. The connection was obvious and nobody had to make it out loud.

But *why*? she thought, feeling nauseated and dizzy. Why would anybody want to drink a girl's blood? No animal and no human did that.

He must be a demon after all.

Arno stepped forward. He gripped Ryl's chin gently, turning her head toward the stranger.

"Was he the one who attacked you?"

Ryl's dazed eyes stared straight ahead—and then she suddenly seemed to focus. Her pupils got big and she looked at the face of the stranger.

Then she started screaming.

Screaming and screaming, hands flying up to cover her eyes. Her mother began to sob, rocking her. Some of the men began to shout at the stranger, jabbing spears at him, overcome with shock and horror. All the sounds merged together in a terrifying cacophony in Hana's head.

Hana found herself trembling. She reached automatically for little Ryl, not knowing how to comfort her. Ket was crying. Sada was wailing as she held her child. People were streaming out of the limestone cave, yelling, trying to find out what all the noise was about.

And through it all, the stranger huddled, his eyes shut, his face a mask of grief.

Arno's voice rose above the others. "I think we hunters know what to do with him. This is no longer a matter for shamans!" He was looking at Hana as he said it.

Hana looked back. She couldn't speak. There was no reason for her to care what happened to the stranger—but she did care. He had hurt her cousin . . . but he was so wretched, so unhappy.

Maybe he couldn't help it, she thought suddenly. She didn't know where the idea came from, but it was the kind of instinct that made Old Mother say she should be a shaman. Maybe . . . he didn't want to do it, but something drove him to. And now he's sorry and ashamed. Maybe . . . oh, I don't know!

Still trembling, she found herself speaking out loud again. "You can't just kill him. You have to take him to Old Mother."

"It's none of her business!"

"It's her business if he's a demon! You're just co-leader, Arno. You take care of the hunting. But Old Mother is the leader in spiritual things."

Arno's face went tight and angry. "Fine, then," he said. "We take him to Old Mother."

Jabbing with their spears, the men drove the stranger into the cave. By then, most of the people of the clan had gathered around and they were muttering angrily.

Old Mother was the oldest woman in the clan—the great grandmother of Hana and Ryl and almost everybody. She had a face covered with wrinkles and a body like a dried stick. But her dark eyes were full of wisdom. She was the clan's shaman. She was the one who interceded directly with the Earth Goddess, the Bright Mother, the Giver of Life who was above all other spirits.

She listened to the story seriously, sitting on her leather pallet while the others crowded around her. Hana edged close to her and Ryl was placed in her lap.

"They want to kill him," Hana murmured in the old woman's ear when the story was over. "But look at his eyes. I know he's sorry, and I think maybe he didn't mean to hurt Ryl. Can you talk to him, Old Mother?"

Old Mother knew a lot of different languages; she'd traveled very far when she had been young. But now, after trying several, she shook her head.

"Demons don't speak human languages," Arno said scornfully. He was standing with his spear ready although the stranger squatting in front of the old woman showed no signs of trying to run away.

"He's not a demon," Old Mother said, with a severe glance at Arno. Then she added slowly, "But he's certainly not a man, either. I'm not sure what he is. The Goddess has never told me anything about people like him."

"Then obviously the Goddess isn't interested," Arno said with a shrug. "Let the hunters take care of him."

Hana gripped the old woman's thin shoulder.

Old Mother put a twiglike hand on Hana's. Her dark eyes were grave and sad.

"The one thing we *do* know is that he's capable of great harm," she said softly. "I'm sorry, child, but I think Arno is right." Then she turned to Arno. "It's getting dark. We'd better shut him up somewhere tonight; then in the morning we can decide what to do with him. Maybe the Goddess will tell me something about him as I sleep."

But Hana knew better. She saw the look on Arno's face as he and the other hunters led the stranger away. And she heard the cold and angry muttering of others in the clan.

In the morning the stranger would die. Unpleasantly, if Arno had his way.

It was probably what he deserved. It was none of Hana's business. But that night, as she lay on her leather pallet underneath her warm furs, she couldn't sleep.

It was as if the Goddess were poking her, telling her that something was wrong. Something had to be done. And there was nobody else to do it.

Hana thought about the look of anguish in the stranger's eyes.

Maybe . . . if he went somewhere far away . . . he couldn't hurt other people. Out on the steppes there were no people to hurt. Maybe that was what the Goddess wanted. Maybe he was some creature that had wandered out of the spirit world and the Goddess would be angry if he were killed.

Hana didn't know; she wasn't a shaman yet. All she knew was that she felt pity for the stranger and she couldn't keep still any longer.

A short time before dawn she got up. Very quietly, she went to the back of the cave and picked up a spare waterskin and some hard patties of traveling food. Then she crept to the side cave where the stranger was shut up.

The hunters had set a sort of fence in front of the cave, like the fences they used to trap animals. It was made of branches and bones lashed together with cords. A hunter was beside the fence, one hand on his spear. He was leaning back against the cave wall, and he was asleep with his mouth open.

Hana edged past him. Her heart was pounding so loudly she was certain it would wake him up. But the hunter didn't move.

Slowly, carefully, Hana pulled one side of the fence outward.

From the darkness inside the cave, two eyes gleamed at her, throwing back the light of the fire.

Hana pressed fingers against her mouth in a sign to be quiet, then beckoned.

It was only then that she realized exactly how dangerous what she was doing was. She was letting him out—what was to stop him from rushing past her and into the main cave, grabbing people and biting them?

But the stranger did no such thing. He didn't move. He sat and his two eyes glowed at Hana.

He's not going to come, she realized. He *won't*.

She beckoned again, more urgently.

The stranger still sat. Hana's eyes were getting used to the darkness in the side cave and now she could see that he was shaking his head. He was determined to stay here and let the clan kill him.

Hana got mad.

Balancing the fence precariously, she jabbed a finger at the stranger, then jerked a thumb over her shoulder. You—out! the gesture meant. She put behind it all the authority of a descendant of Old Mother's, a woman destined to be co-leader of the clan someday.

And when the stranger didn't obey immediately, she reached for him.

That scared him. He shrank back, seeming more alarmed than he had at anything else that had happened so far. He seemed afraid for her to touch him.

Afraid he might hurt me, Hana thought. She didn't know what put the idea into her mind. And she didn't waste time wondering about it. She simply pressed her advantage, reaching for him again, using his fear to make him go where she wanted him to.

She herded him into the main cave and through it. They both moved like shadows among the shelters built along either side of the cave, Hana feeling certain that they were about to be caught any minute. But nobody caught them.

When they got outside she guided him toward the river.

Then she pointed downstream. She put the food and the waterskin in his hands and made far-flung gestures that meant, Go far away. *Very* far away. Very, *very* far. She was going into a pantomime indicating what Arno would do with his spear if the stranger ever came back when she noticed the way he was looking at her.

The moon was up and so bright that she could see every detail of the strange boy's face. And now he was looking at her steadily, with the quiet concentration of a hunting animal, a carnivore. At the same time there was something bleak and terribly human in his eyes.

Hana stopped her pantomime. All at once, the space around the cave seemed very large, and she felt very small. She heard night noises, the croaking of frogs and the rushing of the river, with a peculiar intensity.

I should never have brought him out here. I'm *alone* with him out here. What was I thinking?

There was a long pause while they stood looking at each other silently. The stranger's eyes were very dark, as bottomless and ageless as Old Mother's. Hana could see that his eyelashes were long and she realized again, dimly, that he was handsome.

He lifted the packet of traveling food, looked at it, then with a sudden gesture he threw it on the ground. He did the same with the waterskin. Then he sighed.

Hana was bristling, going from fear to annoyance and back again. What was he doing? Did he think she was trying to poison him? She picked up the food packet, broke a piece of traveling food off and put it in her mouth. Chewing, she extended the packet toward him again. She made gestures from packet to mouth, saying out loud, "You need to eat food. Eat! Eat!"

He was watching her steadily. He took the packet from her, touched his mouth, and shook his head. He dropped it at his feet again.

He means it isn't food to him.

Hana realized it with a shock. She stood and stared at the strange boy.

The food isn't food to him and the water isn't drink. But Ryl's blood . . . he drank that.

Blood is his food and drink.

There was another long pause. Hana was very frightened. Her mouth was trembling and tears had come to her eyes. The stranger was still looking at her quietly, but she could see the fangs indenting his lower lip now and his eyes were reflecting moonlight.

He was looking at her throat.

We're out here alone . . . he could have attacked me at any time, Hana thought. He could attack me right now. He looks very strong. But he hasn't touched me. Even though he's starving, I think. And he looks so grieved, so sad . . . and so hungry.

Her thoughts were tumbling like a piece of bark tossed on the river. She felt very dizzy.

It hurt Ryl . . . but it didn't *kill* Ryl. Ryl was sitting up and eating before we all went to sleep tonight. Old Mother said she's going to get well.

If it didn't kill her, it wouldn't kill me.

Hana swallowed. She looked at the strange boy with the glowing animal eyes. She saw that he wasn't going to move toward her even though a fine trembling had taken over his body and he couldn't seem to look away from her neck.

What good does it do to send him off starving? There's no other clan near here. He'll just have to come back. And I was right before; he doesn't want to do it, but he *has* to do it. Maybe somebody put a curse on him, made it so he starves unless he drinks blood.

There's nobody else to help him.

Very slowly, her eyes on the stranger, Hana lifted the hair from one side of her neck. She exposed her throat, leaning her head back slightly.

Hunger sparked in the strange boy's eyes—and then something blazed in them so quickly and so hot that it swallowed up the hunger. Shock and anger. He was staring at her face, now, not her neck. He shook his head vehemently, glaring.

Hana touched her neck and then her mouth, then made the far-flung gestures. Eat. Then go away.

And for the Goddess's sake, hurry up, she thought, shutting her eyes. Before I panic and change my mind. She was crying now. She couldn't help it. She clenched her fists and her teeth and waited grimly, trying to hang on to her resolve.

When he touched her for the first time, it was to take her hand.

Hana opened her eyes. He was looking at her with such infinite sadness. He smoothed out her fist gently, then kissed her hand. Among any people, it was a gesture of gratitude . . . and reverence.

And it sent startling tingles through Hana. A feeling that was almost like shivers, but warm. A lightness in her head and a weakness in her legs. A sense of awe and wonder that she'd only ever felt before when Old Mother was teaching her to communicate with the Goddess.

She could see startled reaction in the stranger's eyes, too. He was feeling the same things, and they were equally new to him. Hana *knew* that. But then he dropped her hand quickly and she knew that he was also afraid. The feelings were dangerous—because they drew the two of them together.

One long moment while they stood and she saw moonlight in his eyes.

Then he turned to go.

Hana watched him, her throat aching, knowing he was going to die.

And somehow that wrenched her insides in a way she'd never experienced before. Although she kept herself standing still, with her head high, she could feel the tears running down her cheeks. She didn't know why she felt this way—but it hurt her terribly. It was as if she were losing something . . . infinitely precious . . . before she'd had a chance to know it.

The future seemed gray, now. Empty. Lonely.

Cold and desolate, she stood by the rushing river and felt the wind blow through her. So alone . . .

"Hannah! Hannah! Wake up!"

Someone was shouting, but it wasn't a voice from her cave. It sounded—faraway—and seemed to come from all directions, or maybe from the sky itself.

And it was saying her name wrong.

"Hannah, wake up! Please! Open your eyes!" The faraway voice was frantic.

And then there was another voice, a quiet voice that seemed to strike a chord deep inside Hana. A voice that was even less like sound, and that spoke in Hana's mind.

Hannah, come back. You don't have to relive all this. Wake up. Come back, Hannah—now.

Hana of the Three Rivers closed her eyes and went limp.

CHAPTER 6

Hannah opened her eyes.

"Oh, thank God," Paul said. He seemed to be almost crying. "Oh, thank God. Do you see me? Do you know who you are?"

"I'm wet," Hannah said slowly, feeling dazed. She touched her face. Her hair was dripping. Paul was holding a water glass. "Why am I wet?"

"I had to wake you up." Paul sagged to the floor beside the couch. "What's your name? What year is it?"

"My name is Hannah Snow," Hannah said, still feeling dazed and bodiless. "And it's—" Suddenly memory rushed out of the fog at her. She sat bolt upright, tears starting to stream from her eyes. "What *was* all that?"

"I don't know," Paul whispered. He leaned his head against the couch, then looked up. "You just kept talking—you were telling that story as if you were there. It was really *happening* to you. And nothing I could do would break the trance. I tried everything—I thought you were never going to come out of it. And then you started sobbing and I couldn't make you stop."

"I *felt* as if it were happening to me," Hannah said. Her head ached; her whole body felt bruised with tension. And she was reeling with memories that were perfectly real and perfectly hers . . . and impossible.

"That was like no past life regression I've ever read about," Paul said, his voice agitated. "The detail . . . you knew everything. Have you ever studied—is there any way you could have known those kinds of things?"

"No." Hannah was just as agitated. "I've never studied humans in the Stone Age—and this was *real.* It wasn't something I was making up as I was going along."

They were both talking at once. "That guy," Paul was saying. "He's the one you're afraid of, isn't he? But, look, you know, regression is one thing . . . past lives is another thing . . . but *this* is crazy."

"I don't believe in vampires," Hannah was saying at the same time. "Because that's what that guy was supposed to be, wasn't it? Of course it was. Caveman vampire. He was probably the first one. And I don't believe in reincarnation."

"Just plain crazy. This is crazy."

"I *agree.*"

They both took a breath, looking at each other. There was a long silence.

Hannah put a hand to her forehead. "I'm . . . really tired."

"Yeah. Yeah, I can understand that." Paul looked around the room, nodded twice, then got up. "Well, we'd better get you home. We can talk about all this later, figure out what it really means. Some kind of subconscious fixation . . . archetypical symbolism . . . something." He ran out of air and shook his head. "Now, you feel all right, don't you? And you're not going to worry about this? Because there's nothing to worry about."

"I know. I know."

"At least we know we don't have to worry about vampires attacking you." He laughed. The laugh was strained.

Hannah couldn't manage even a smile.

There was a brief silence, then Paul said, "You know, I think I'll drive you home. That would be good. That would be a good idea."

"That would be fine," Hannah whispered.

He held out a hand to help her off the couch. "By the way, I'm really sorry I had to get you all wet."

"No. It was good you did. I was feeling so awful—and there were worse things about to happen."

Paul blinked. "I'm sorry?"

Hannah looked at him helplessly, then away. "There were worse things about to happen. Terrible things. Really, really awful things."

"How do you know that?"

"I don't know. But there were."

Paul walked her to her doorstep. And Hannah was glad of it.

Once inside the house, she went straight down the hall to her mother's study. It was a cluttered, comfortable room with books piled on the floor and the tools of a paleontologist scattered around. Her mother was at her desk, bending over a microscope.

"Is that you, Hannah?" she asked without looking up. "I've got some marvelous sections of haversian canals in duckbill bones. Want to see?"

"Oh . . . not now. Maybe later," Hannah said. She wanted very much to tell her mother about what had happened, but something was stopping her. Her mother was so sensible, so practical and intelligent. . . .

She'll think I'm crazy. And she'll be right. And then she'll be appalled, wondering how she could have given birth to an insane daughter.

That was an exaggeration, and Hannah knew it, but somehow she still couldn't bring herself to tell. Since her father had died five years ago, she and her mother had been almost like friends—but that didn't mean she didn't want her mother's approval. She did. She desperately wanted her mother to be proud of her, and to realize that she could handle things on her own.

It had been the same with the notes—she'd never told about finding them. For all her mom knew, Hannah's only problem was bad dreams.

"So how did it go tonight?" her mother asked now, eye still to the microscope. "That Dr. Winfield is so young—I hope he's not too inexperienced."

Last chance. Take it or lose it. "Uh, it went fine," Hannah said weakly.

"That's good. There's chicken in the crockpot. I'll be out in a little while; I just want to finish this."

"Okay. Great. Thanks." Hannah turned and stumbled out, completely frustrated with herself.

You know Mom won't really be awful, she scolded herself as she fished a piece of chicken out of the crockpot. So *tell* her. Or call Chess and tell *her*. They'll make things better. They'll tell you how impossible all this stuff about vampires and past lives is. . . .

Yes, and that's the problem.

Hannah sat frozen, holding a fork with a bite of chicken on it motionless in front of her.

I don't believe in vampires or reincarnation. But I know what I saw. I know things about Hana . . . things that weren't even in the story I told Paul. I know she wore a tunic and leggings of roe deer hide. I know she ate wild cattle and wild boar and salmon and hazelnuts. I know she made tools out of elk antler and deer bone and flint. . . . God, I could pick up a flint cobble and knock off a set of blades and scrapers right now. I *know* I could. I can feel how to in my hands.

She put the fork down and looked at her hands. They were shaking slightly.

And I know she had a beautiful singing voice, a voice like crystal. . . .

Like the crystal voice in my mind.

So what do I do when they tell me it's impossible? Argue with them? Then I'll *really* be crazy, like those people in institutions who think they're Napoleon or Cleopatra.

God, I hope I haven't been Cleopatra.

Half laughing and half crying, she put her face in her hands.

And what about *him*?

The blond stranger with the bottomless eyes. The guy Hana didn't have a name for, but Hannah knew as Thierry.

If the rest of it is real, what about him?

He's the one I'm afraid of, Hannah thought. But he didn't seem so bad. Dangerous, but not evil. So why do I think of him as evil?

And why do I want him anyway?

Because she did want him. She remembered the feelings of Hana standing next to the stranger in the moonlight. Confusion . . . fear . . . and attraction. That magnetism between them. The extraordinary things that happened when he touched her hand.

He came to the Three Rivers and turned her life upside down. . . . *The Three Rivers*. Oh, God—why didn't I think of that before? The *note*. One of the notes said "Remember the Three Rivers."

Okay. So I've remembered it. So what now?

She had no idea. Maybe she was supposed to understand everything now, and know what to do . . . but she didn't. She was more confused than ever.

Of course, a tiny voice like a cool dark wind in her brain said, you didn't remember *all* of it yet. Did you? Paul woke you up before you got to the end.

Shut up, Hannah told the voice.

But she couldn't stop thinking. All night she was restless, moving from one room to another, avoiding her mother's questions. And even after her mother went to bed, Hannah found herself wandering aimlessly through the house, straightening things, picking up books and putting them down again.

I've got to sleep. That's the only thing that will help me feel better, she thought. But she couldn't make herself sit, much less lie down.

Maybe I need some air.

It was a strange thought. She'd never actually felt the need to go outside for the sole purpose of breathing fresh air—in Montana you did that all day long. But there was something pulling at her, drawing her to go outside. It was like a compulsion and she couldn't resist.

I'll just go on the back porch. Of course there's nothing to be scared of out there. And if I go outside, then I'll *prove* there isn't, and then I can go to sleep.

Without stopping to consider the logic of this, she opened the back door.

It was a beautiful night. The moon threw a silver glow over everything and the horizon seemed very far away. Hannah's backyard blended into the wild bluestem and pine grass of the prairie. The wind carried the clean pungent smell of sage.

We'll have spring flowers soon, Hannah thought. Asters and bluebells and little golden buttercups. Everything will be green for a while. Spring's a time for life, not death.

And I was right to come out. I feel more relaxed now. I can go back inside and lie down. . . .

It was at that moment that she realized she was being watched.

It was the same feeling she'd been having for weeks, the feeling that there were eyes in the darkness and they were fixed on her. Chills of adrenaline ran through Hannah's body.

Don't panic, she told herself. It's just a feeling. There's probably nothing out here.

She took a slow step backward toward the door. She didn't want to move too quickly. She had the irrational certainty that if she turned and ran, whatever was watching her would spring out and get her before she got the door open.

At the same time she edged backward, her eyes and ears

were straining so hard that she saw gray spots and she heard a thin ringing. She was trying, desperately, to catch some sign of movement, some sound. But everything was still and the only noises were the normal distant noises of the outdoors.

Then she saw the shadow.

Black against the lighter blackness of the night, it was moving among the bluestem grass. And it was big. Tall. Not a cat or other small animal. Big as a person.

It was coming toward her.

Hannah thought she might faint.

Don't be ridiculous, a sharp voice in her head told her. Get *inside*. You're standing here in the light from the windows; you're a perfect target. Get inside *fast* and lock the door.

Hannah whirled, and knew even as she did it that she wouldn't be fast enough. It was going to jump at her exposed back. It was going to . . .

"Wait," came a voice out of the darkness. "Please. Wait."

A male voice. Unfamiliar. But it seemed to grab Hannah and hold her still.

"I won't hurt you. I promise."

Runrunrunrun! Hannah's mind told her.

Very slowly, one hand on the doorknob, she turned around.

She watched the dark figure coming out of the shadows to her. She didn't try to get away again. She had a dizzying feeling that fate had caught up with her.

The ground sloped, so the light from the house windows showed her his boots first, then the legs of his jeans. Normal walking boots like any Montanan might wear. Ordinary jeans—long legs. He was tall. Then the light showed his shirt, which was an ordinary T-shirt, a little cold to be walking around at night in, but nothing startling. And then his shoulders, which were nice ones.

Then, as he stepped to the base of the porch, she saw his face.

He looked better than when she had seen him last. His white-blond hair wasn't crazily messed up; it fell neatly over his forehead. He wasn't splattered with mud and his eyes weren't wild. They were dark and so endlessly sad that it was like a knife in the heart just to see him.

But it was unmistakably the boy from her hypnosis session.

"Oh, God," Hannah said. "Oh, God." Her knees were giving out.

It's real. It's *real*. He's real and that means . . . it's all true.

"Oh, *God*." She was trembling violently and she had to put pressure on her knees to keep standing. The world was changing around her, and it was the most disorienting thing she'd ever experienced. It was as if the fabric of her universe was actually moving—pulsing and shifting to accommodate the new truths.

Nothing was ever going to be the same again.

"Are you all right?" The stranger moved toward her and Hannah recoiled instinctively.

"Don't touch me!" she gasped, and at the same moment her legs gave out. She slid to the floor of the porch and stared at the boy whose face was now approximately level with hers.

"I'm sorry," he almost whispered. "I know what you're going through. You're just realizing now, aren't you?"

Hannah said, whispering to herself, "It's all true."

"Yes." The dark eyes were so sad.

"It's . . . I've had past lives."

"Yes." He squatted on the ground, looking down as if he couldn't keep staring at her face anymore. He picked up a pebble, examined it. Hannah noticed that his fingers were long and sensitive-looking.

"You're an Old Soul," he said quietly. "You've had lots of lives."

"I was Hana of the Three Rivers."

His fingers stopped rolling the pebble. "Yes."

"And you're Thierry. And you're a . . ."

He didn't look up. "Go on. Say it."

Hannah couldn't. Her voice wouldn't form the word.

The stranger—Thierry—said it for her. "Vampires are real." A glance from those unfathomable eyes. "I'm sorry."

Hannah breathed and looked down at him. But the world had finished its reshaping. Her mind was beginning to work again.

At least I know I'm not crazy, she thought. That's some consolation. It's the universe that's insane, not me.

And now I have to deal with it—somehow.

She said quietly, "Are you going to kill me now?"

"God—no!" He stood up fast, uncoiling. Shock was naked on his face. "You don't understand. I would never hurt you. I . . ." He broke off. "It's hard to know where to begin."

Hannah sat silently, while he looked around the porch for inspiration. She could feel her heart beating in her throat. She'd told Paul that this boy had killed her, kept killing her. But his look of shock had been so genuine—as if she'd hurt him terribly by even suggesting it.

"I suppose I should start by explaining exactly what I am," he said. "And what I've done. I made you come outside tonight. I influenced you. I didn't want to do it, but I had to talk to you."

"Influenced me?"

It's a mental thing. I can also just communicate this way. It was his voice, but his lips weren't moving.

And it was the same voice she'd heard at the end of her hypnotic session, the voice that wasn't Paul's. The one that had spoken in her head, saying, *Hannah, come back. You don't have to relive this.*

"You were the one who woke me up," Hannah whispered. "I wouldn't have come back except for you."

"I couldn't stand to see you hurting like that."

Can somebody with his eyes be evil?

He was obviously a different sort of creature than she was, and every move he made showed the grace of a predator. It reminded her of how the wolves had moved—they had *rippled.*

He did, too, his muscles moving so lightly under his skin. He was unnatural—but beautiful.

Something struck her. "The wolves. I picked up a silver picture frame to bash them with. Silver." She looked at him. "Werewolves are real." At the last moment her voice made it a statement instead of a question.

"So much is real that you don't know about. Or that you haven't remembered yet. You were starting to remember with that shrink. You said I was a Lord of the Night World."

The Night World. Just the mention of it sent prickles through Hannah. She could almost remember, but not quite.

And she knew it was crazy to be kneeling here having this conversation. She was talking to a *vampire.* A guy who drank blood for a living. A guy whose every gesture showed he was a hunter. And not only a vampire, but the person her subconscious had been warning her about for weeks. Telling her to be afraid, be very afraid.

So why wasn't she running? For one thing, she didn't think her legs would physically support her. And for another—well, somehow she couldn't stop looking at him.

"One of the werewolves was mine," he was saying quietly. "She was here to find you—and protect you. But the other one . . . Hannah, you have to understand. I'm not the only one looking for you."

To protect me. So I was right, Hannah thought. The gray female was on my side. She said, "Who else is looking?"

"Another Night Person." He looked away. "Another vampire."

"Am I a Night Person?"

"No. You're a human." He said it the way he said every-thing, as if reminding her of terrible facts he wished he didn't have to bring up. "Old Souls are just humans who keep com-ing back."

"How many times have I come back?"

"I . . . I'd have to think about it. Quite a few."

"And have *you* been with me in all of them?"

"Any of them I could manage."

"What do the rest of the notes mean?" Hannah had been gathering speed, and now she was shooting questions at him in machine-gun fashion. She thought she was in control, and she hardly noticed the hysterical edge to her own voice. "*Why* am I telling myself I'll be dead before I'm seventeen?"

"Hannah . . ." He reached out a hand to calm her.

Hannah's own hand moved by reflex, coming up to ward his off. And then their fingers touched, bare skin to bare skin, and the world disappeared.

CHAPTER 7

It was like being struck by lightning. Hannah felt the current through her body, but it was her mind that was most affected.

I know you! It was as if she had been standing in a dark landscape, lost and blind, when suddenly a brilliant flash illuminated everything, allowing her to see farther than she'd ever seen before. She was trembling violently, pitching forward even as he fell toward her. Electricity was running through every nerve in her body and she was shaking and shaking, overcome by waves of the purest emotion she'd ever felt.

Fury.

"You were supposed to be there!" She got out in a choked gasp. "Where *were* you?"

You were supposed to be with me—for so long! You're *part* of me, the part I've always vaguely missed. You were supposed to be around, helping out, picking me up when I fell down.

Watching my back, listening to my stories. Understanding things that I wouldn't want to tell other people. Loving me when I'm stupid. Giving *me* something to take care of and be good to, the way the Goddess meant women to do.

Hannah—

It was the closest thing to a mental gasp Hannah could imagine, and with it she realized that somehow they were directly connected now. He could hear her thoughts, just as she could hear his.

Good! she thought, not wasting time to marvel over this. Her mind was raging on.

You were my flying companion! My playmate! You were my other half of the mysteries! We were supposed to be sacred to each other—*and you haven't been there!*

This last thought she sent squarely toward him. And she felt it hit him, and felt his reaction.

"I've *tried*!"

He was horrified . . . guilt-stricken. But then, Hannah could sense that this was pretty much the usual state for him, so it didn't affect him quite as much as it might have someone else. And beneath the horror was an astonishment and burgeoning joy that sent a different kind of tingle through her.

"You *do* know me, don't you?" he said quietly. He pushed her back to look at her, as if he still couldn't believe it. "You remember . . . Hannah, how much do you remember?"

Hannah was looking at him, studying him. . . . Yes, I know that bone structure. And the eyes, especially the eyes. It was like an adopted child discovering a brother or sister and seeing familiar features in an unfamiliar face, tracing each one with wonder and recognition.

"I remember . . . that we were meant for each other. That we're"—she came up with the word slowly—"*soulmates.*"

"Yes," he whispered. Awe was softening his features, changing his eyes. The desperate sadness that seemed so much a part of them was lightening. "Soulmates. We were destined for each other. We should have been together down the ages."

They were supporting each other now, Hannah kneeling on the porch and Thierry holding her with one knee on a step. Their faces were inches apart. Hannah found herself watching his mouth.

"So what happened?" she whispered.

In the same tone, without moving back, he whispered, "I screwed up."

"Oh."

Her initial fury had faded. She could *feel* him, feel his emotions, sense his thoughts. He was as anguished at their separation as she was. He wanted her. He loved her . . . adored her. He thought of her the way poets think of the moon and the stars—in ridiculous hyperbole. He actually saw her surrounded by a sort of silvery halo.

Which was completely silly, but if he wanted to think of her that way—well, Hannah wouldn't object. It made her want to be very gentle with him.

And right now she could feel his warm breath. If she leaned forward just an inch her top lip would touch his bottom lip.

Hannah leaned forward.

"Wait—" he said.

That was a mistake, saying it out loud. It moved his lips against hers, turning it from a touch into a kiss.

And then, for a while, neither of them could resist. They needed each other so desperately, and the kiss was warm and sweet. Hannah was flooded with love and comfort and joy.

This was meant to be.

Hannah was dizzy but still capable of thought. *I knew life had something wonderful and mysterious to give me. Something I could sense but not see, something that was always just out of reach.*

And here it is. I'm one of the lucky ones—I've found it.

Thierry wasn't as articulate. All she could hear him think was, *Yes.*

Hannah had never been so filled with gratitude. Love spilled from her and into Thierry and back again. The more she gave, the more she got back. It was a cycle, taking them higher and higher.

Like flying, Hannah thought. She wasn't dizzy anymore. She was strangely clear and calm, as if she were standing on a mountaintop. Infinite tenderness . . . infinite belonging. It was so good it hurt.

And it made her want to give more.

She knew what she wanted. It was what she'd tried to give him the first time, when she knew he would die without her. She'd wanted to give him what all women could give.

Life.

She was only a girl now, not ready for the responsibilities that would come with making new life from her body. But she could give Thierry life another way.

She pulled back to look at him, to see bruised dark eyes filled with aching tenderness. Then she touched his mouth with her fingertips.

He kissed them. Hannah ignored the kiss and poked a finger in.

Shock flared in Thierry's eyes.

There. That was it. The long canine tooth, just barely sharp. Not yet the tooth of a predator, of a fox or a lynx or wolf. She ran her finger against it.

The shock turned to something else. A glazed look. Need mixed with pure terror.

Thierry whispered, "Don't—Hannah, please. You don't know—"

Hannah tested the tip of the tooth with her thumb. Yes, it was sharper now. Longer, more delicate. It would look like the tooth of an arctic fox in her palm—milky-white, translucent, elegantly curved.

Thierry's chest was heaving. "Please stop. I—I can't—"

Hannah was enthralled. I don't know why people are afraid of vampires, she thought. A human could tease or torture a vampire this way, driving him insane—if she were cruel.

Or she could choose to be kind.

Very gently, Hannah reached with her other hand. She touched the back of Thierry's neck, bringing just the slightest pressure to bear. But he was so obedient to her touch—it was easy to guide his mouth to her throat.

Hannah . . .

She could feel him trembling.

Don't be afraid, she told him silently. And she pulled him closer.

He grabbed her shoulders to push her away—and then just hung on. Clinging desperately, helplessly. Kissing her neck over and over. She felt his control break . . . and then felt the sharpness of teeth.

It wasn't like pain. It was like the tenderness, a hurting that was good.

And then . . . devastating bliss.

Not a physical feeling. It was emotional. They were completely together, and light poured through them.

How many lives together have we missed? How many

times have I had to say, Maybe in the next life? How did we ever manage to come apart?

It was as if her question went searching through both their minds, soaring and diving, looking for an answer on its own. And Thierry didn't put up any resistance. She knew that he couldn't; he was as caught up as she was in what was happening between them, as overwhelmed.

There was nothing to stop her from finding the answer.

This revelation didn't come all in one blinding illumination. Instead it came in small flashes, each almost too brief to understand.

Flash. Thierry's face above her. Not the gentle face she had seen by the porch. A savage face with an animal light in the eyes. A snarling mouth . . . and teeth red with blood.

No . . .

Flash. Pain. Teeth that tore her throat. The feel of her blood spilling warm over her neck. Darkness coming.

Oh, God, no . . .

Flash. A different face. A woman with black hair and eyes full of concern. "Don't you know? He's evil. How many times does he have to kill you before you realize that?"

No, no, no, no . . .

But saying no didn't change anything.

It was the truth. She was seeing her own memories—seeing things that had really happened. She *knew* that.

He'd killed her.

Hannah, no—

It was a cry of anguish. Hannah wrenched herself away. She could see the shock in Thierry's eyes, she could feel him shaking.

"You really did it," she whispered.

"Hannah—"

"That's why you woke me up from the hypnosis! You didn't want me to remember! You knew I'd find out the truth!" Hannah was beside herself with grief and anger. If she hadn't trusted him, if everything hadn't been so perfect, she wouldn't have felt so betrayed. As it was, it was the greatest betrayal of her life—of all her lives.

It had all been a lie—everything she'd just been feeling. The togetherness, the love, the joy . . . all false.

"Hannah, that wasn't the reason. . . ."

"You're evil! You're a killer!" *She told me,* Hannah thought. *The woman with black hair; she told me the truth. Why didn't I remember her? Why didn't I listen this time?*

She could remember other things now, other things the woman had said. "He's unbelievably cunning . . . he'll try to trick you. He'll try to use mind control . . ."

Mind control. Influencing her. He'd *admitted* that.

And what she'd been feeling tonight was some sort of trick. He'd managed to play on her emotions . . . God, he'd even gotten her to offer him her blood. She'd let him *bite* her, drink from her like some parasite. . . .

"I hate you," she whispered.

She saw how that hurt him; he flinched and looked away, stricken. Then he gripped her shoulders again, his voice soft. "Hannah, I wanted to explain to you. Please. You don't understand everything . . ."

"Yes, I do! I *do*! I remember everything! And I understand what you really are." Her voice was as quiet as his, but much more intense. She shrugged her shoulders and shifted backward to get away from him. She didn't want to feel his hands on her.

He looked jolted. Unbelieving. "You remember . . . everything?"

"Everything." Hannah was proud and cold now. "So you can just go away, because whatever you've got planned won't work. Whatever—tricks—you were going to use . . ." She shook her head. "Just go."

For just a second, a strange expression crossed Thierry's face. An expression so tragic and lonely that Hannah's throat closed.

But she couldn't let herself soften. She couldn't give him a chance to trick her again.

"Just stay away from me," she said. With all the confusion and turmoil inside her, that was the only thing she could keep clear in her mind. "I never want to see you again."

He had gotten control of himself. He looked shell-shocked but his eyes were steady. "I've never wanted to hurt you," he said quietly. "And all I want to do now is protect you. But if that's what you want, I'll go away."

How could he claim he'd never wanted to hurt her? Didn't killing her count? "That *is* what I want. And I don't need your protection."

"You have it anyway," he said.

And then he moved, faster than she could ever hope to move, almost faster than thought. In an instant, he was close to her. His fingers touched her left cheek, light as a moth's wings. And then he was taking her hand, slipping something on her finger.

"Wear this," he said, no louder than a breath. "It has spells to protect you. And even without the spells, there aren't many Night People who'll harm you if they see it."

Hannah opened her mouth to say she wasn't afraid of any Night People except him, but he was still speaking. "Try not to go out alone, especially at night."

And then he was gone.

Like that. He was off her porch and out somewhere in the darkness, not even a shadow, just *gone.* If she hadn't had a fleeting impression of movement toward the prairie, she would have thought he had the ability to become invisible at a moment's notice.

And her heart was pounding, hurting, filling her throat so she couldn't breathe.

Why had he touched her cheek? Most people didn't touch

the birthmark; they treated it like a bruise that might still hurt. But his fingers hadn't avoided it. The caress had been gentle, almost sad, but not frightened.

And why was she still standing here, staring into the darkness as if she expected him to reappear?

Go *inside,* idiot.

Hannah turned and fumbled with the back door, pulling at the knob as if she'd never opened it before. She shut the door and locked it, and again she found herself as clumsy as if she'd never worked a lock or seen this one in her life.

She was beyond screaming or crying, in a state of shock that was almost dreamlike. The house was too bright. The clock on the kitchen wall was too loud. She had the distracted feeling that it wasn't either night or daytime.

It was like coming out of a theater and being surprised to find that it's still light outside. She felt that this couldn't be the same house she'd left an hour ago. *She* wasn't the same person who had left. Everything around her seemed like some carefully staged movie set that was supposed to be real, but wasn't, and only she could tell the difference.

I feel like a stranger here, she thought, putting one hand to her neck where she could just detect two little puncture marks. Oh, God, how am I ever going to know what's real again?

But I should be happy; I should be grateful. I probably just saved my own life out there. I was alone with a vicious, evil, murderous monster, and . . .

Somehow the thought died away. She couldn't be happy and she didn't want to think about how evil Thierry was. She felt hollow and aching.

It wasn't until she stumbled into her own bedroom that she remembered to look down at her right hand.

On the fourth finger was a ring. It was made of gold and either white gold or silver. It was shaped like a rose, with the stem twining around the finger and back on itself in an intricate knot. The blossom was inset with tiny stones—black transparent stones. Black diamonds? Hannah wondered.

It was beautiful. The craftsmanship was exquisite. Every delicate leaf and tiny thorn was perfect. But a black flower?

It's a symbol of the Night World, her mind told her. A symbol of people who've been made into vampires.

It was the cool wind voice back again. At least she understood what it was saying this time—the last time, when it had given her advice about silver and wolves, she had been completely confused.

Thierry wanted her to wear the ring; he claimed it would protect her. But knowing him, it was probably another trick. If it had any spells on it, they were probably spells to help him control her mind.

It took nearly an hour to get the ring off. Hannah used soap and butter and Vaseline, pulling and twisting until her finger was red, aching, and swollen. She used a dental pick from her fossil-collecting kit to try to pry the coils of the stem apart. Nothing worked, until at last the pick slipped and blood welled up from a shallow cut. When the blood touched the ring it seemed to loosen, and Hannah quickly wrenched it off.

Then she stood panting. The struggle with the little band of metal had left her exhausted and unable to focus on anything else. She threw the ring in her bedroom wastebasket and stumbled toward bed.

I'm tired . . . I'm so tired. I'll think about everything tomorrow, try to sort out my life. But for now . . . please just let me sleep.

She could feel her body vibrating with adrenaline after she lay in bed, and she was afraid that sleep wouldn't come. But tense as she was, her mind was too foggy to stay awake. She turned over once and let go of consciousness. Hannah Snow fell asleep.

Hana of the Three Rivers opened her eyes.

Cold and desolate, Hana stood by the rushing river and felt the wind blow through her. So alone.

That was when Arno burst out of the bushes on the riverbank.

There were several hunters with him and they all had spears. They charged after the stranger at full speed. Hana screamed a warning, but she knew he didn't have a chance.

She could hear a few minutes of chaos far away in the dark.

And then she saw the stranger being driven back, surrounded by Arno's hunters.

"Arno—don't hurt him! Please!" Hana was speaking desperately, trying to block the men's way back. "Don't you see? He could have hurt me and he didn't. He isn't a demon! He can't help being the way he is!"

Arno shouldered her aside. "Don't think you're going to get away without being punished, either."

Hana followed them up to the cave, her stomach churning with fear.

By the time everyone who'd been awakened by Arno's hunters understood what was happening, the sky outside had turned gray. It was almost dawn.

"You said we should wait and see if the Earth Goddess would tell you something about the demon while you slept," Arno said to Old Mother. "Has she?"

Old Mother glanced at Hana sorrowfully, then back at Arno. She shook her head. Then she started to speak, but Arno was already talking loudly.

"Then let's kill him and get it over with. Take him outside."

"*No!*" Hana screamed. It didn't do any good. She was caught and held back in strong hands. The stranger gave her one look as he was driven outside in a circle of spears.

That was when the real horror began.

Because of something that Hana had never imagined,

something she was sure even the shamans had never heard of.

The stranger was a creature that wouldn't die.

Arno was the first to jab with his spear. The whitish-gray flint spearhead went into the stranger's side, drawing blood. Hana saw it; she had run out of the cave, still trying to find a way to stop this.

She also saw the blood stop flowing as the wound in the boy's side closed.

There were gasps from all around her. Arno, looking as if he couldn't believe his eyes, jabbed again. And watched, mouth falling open, as the second wound bled and then closed. He kept trying. Only the wounds where a spear was driven into the wooden shaft stayed open.

One of the women whispered, "He *is* a demon."

Everyone was frightened. But nobody moved away from the stranger. He was too dangerous to let go. And there were lots of them, and only one of him.

Hana saw something happening in the faces of her clan. Something new and horrible. Fear of the unknown was changing them, making them cruel. They were turning from basically good people, people who would never torture an animal by prolonging its death, into people who would torture a man.

"He may be a demon, but he still bleeds," one of the hunters said breathlessly, after a jab. "He feels pain."

"Get a torch," somebody else said. "See if he burns!"

And then it was terrible. Hana felt as if she were in the

middle of a storm, able to see things but buffeted this way and that, unable to *do* anything about it. People were running. People were getting torches, stone axes, different kinds of flint knives. The clan had turned into a huge entity feeding off its own violence. It was mindless and unstoppable.

Hana cast a desperate look toward the cave, where Old Mother lay confined to her pallet. There was no help from that direction.

People were screaming, burning the stranger, throwing stones at him. The stranger was falling, bloody, smoke rising from his burns. He was lying on the ground, unable to fight back. But still, he didn't die. He kept trying to crawl away.

Hana was screaming herself, screaming and crying, beating at the shoulders of a hunter who pulled her back. And it went on and on. Even the young boys were brave enough now to run forward and throw stones at the stranger.

And he still wouldn't die.

Hana was in a nightmare. Her throat was raw from screaming. Her vision was going gray. She couldn't stand to watch this anymore; she couldn't stand the smell of blood and burning flesh or the sound of blows. But there was nowhere to go. There was no way to get out. This was her life. She had to stay here and go insane. . . .

CHAPTER 8

Hannah sat up in bed, gasping.

For several moments she didn't know where she was. Through a gap in her curtains she could see the gray light of dawn—just like Hana's gray dawn—and she thought she still might be in the nightmare. But then, slowly, objects in the room became clear. Her bookshelves, crammed with books and crowned with one near-perfect trilobite fossil on a stand. Her dresser, its top piled with things that belonged in other places. Her posters of *Velociraptor* and *T. rex*.

I'm me. I remember me.

She had never been so happy to be herself, or to be awake.

But that dream she'd just had—that had happened to her. A long time ago, sure, but nothing like so long ago as, say, when the *T. rex* had been alive. Not to mention the trilobite. A few thousand years was yesterday to Mother Earth.

And it was all real, she knew that now. She accepted it.

She had fallen asleep and her subconscious had pulled back the veil of the past and allowed her to see more of Hana's story.

Thierry, she thought. The people of Hana's clan tortured him. God knows for how long—I'm just glad I didn't have to watch more.

But it puts sort of a different twist on things, doesn't it?

She still didn't know how the story ended. She wasn't sure she *wanted* to know. But it was hard to blame him for whatever had happened afterward.

An awful feeling was settling in Hannah's stomach. All those things I said to him—terrible things, she thought. Why did I say all that? I was so angry—I lost control completely. I hated him and all I cared about was hurting him. I really thought he must be evil, pure evil.

I told him to go away forever.

How could I have done that? He's my soulmate.

There was a strange emptiness inside her, as if she'd been hollowed out like a tree struck by lightning.

Inside the emptiness, a voice like a cool dark wind whispered, But you told Paul that he kept killing you over and over. Is *that* justifiable? He's a vampire, a predator, and that makes him evil by nature. Maybe he can't help being what he is, but there's no reason for you to be destroyed again because of it. Are you going to let him kill you in this life, too?

She was torn between pity for him and the deep instinct

that he was dangerous. The cool wind voice seemed to be the voice of reason.

Go ahead and feel sorry for him, it said. Just keep him far away from you.

She felt better having come to a decision, even if it was a decision that left her heart numb. She glanced around the room, focused on the clock by her bedside, and blinked.

Oh, my God—school.

It was quarter to seven and it was a Friday. Sacajawea High seemed light-years away, like someplace she'd visited in a past life.

But it's not. It's *your* life now, the only one that counts. You have to forget all that other stuff about reincarnation and vampires and the Night World. You have to forget about *him*.

You sent him away and he's gone. So let's get on with living in the normal world.

Just thinking this way made her feel braced and icy, as if she'd had a cold shower. She took a real shower, dressed in jeans and a denim shirt, and she had breakfast with her mother, who cast her several thoughtful glances but didn't ask any questions until they were almost finished.

Then she said, "Did everything go all right at Dr. Winfield's yesterday evening?"

Had it only been yesterday evening? It seemed like a week ago. Hannah chewed a bite of cornflakes and finally said, "Uh, why?"

"Because he called while you were in the shower. He seemed . . ." Her mother stopped and searched for a word. "*Anxious.* Worse than worried but not as bad as hysterical."

Hannah looked at her mother's face, which was narrow, intelligent, and tanned by the Montana sun. Her eyes were more blue than Hannah's gray, but they were direct and discerning.

She wanted to tell her mother the whole story—but when she had time to do it, and after she'd had time to think it out. There was no urgency. It was all behind her now, and it wasn't as if she needed advice.

"Paul's anxious a lot," she said judiciously, sticking to the clean edge of truth. "I think that's why he became a psychologist. He tried a sort of hypnosis thing on me yesterday and it didn't exactly work out."

"Hypnosis?" Her mother's eyebrows lifted. "Hannah, I don't know if you should be getting into that—"

"Don't worry; I'm not. It's over. We're not going to try it again."

"I see. Well, he said for you to call him to set up another appointment. I think he wants to see you soon." She reached over suddenly and took Hannah's hand. "Honey, are you feeling any *better*? Are you still having bad dreams?"

Hannah looked away. "Actually—I sort of had one last night. But I think I understand them better now. They don't scare me as much." She squeezed her mother's hand. "Don't worry, I'm going to be fine."

"All right, but—" Before her mother could finish the sentence a horn honked outside.

"That's Chess. I'd better run." Hannah gulped down the dregs of her orange juice and dashed into her bedroom to grab her backpack. She hesitated a split second by the wastebasket, then shook her head.

No. There was no reason to take the black rose ring with her. It was *his*, and she didn't want to be reminded of him.

She slung the backpack over her shoulder, yelled goodbye to her mother, and hurried outside.

Chess's car was parked in the driveway. As Hannah started toward it she had an odd impression. She seemed to see a figure standing behind the car—a tall figure, face turned toward her. But her eyes were dazzled by the sun and at that instant she involuntarily blinked. When she could see again, there was nothing in that spot except a little swirl of dust.

"You're late," Chess said when Hannah got in the car. Chess, whose real name was Catherine Clovis, was petite and pretty, with dark hair cut in a cap to frame her face. But just now her slanted green cat eyes and Mona Lisa smile reminded Hannah too much of Ket. It was disconcerting; she had to glance down to make sure Chess wasn't wearing a deerskin outfit.

"You okay?" Now Chess was looking at her with concern.

"Yeah." Hannah sank back against the upholstery, blinking. "I think I need to get my eyes checked, though." She glanced at the spot where the phantom figure had been—nothing. And Chess was just Chess: smart, savvy, and faintly exotic, like an orchid blooming in the badlands.

"Well, you can do it when we go shopping this weekend," Chess said. She slanted Hannah a glance. "We *must* go shopping. Next week's your birthday and I need something new to wear."

Hannah grinned in spite of herself. "Maybe a new necklace," she muttered.

"What?"

"Nothing." I wonder what happened to Ket, she thought. Even if Hana died young, at least Ket must have grown up. I wonder if she married Ran, the guy who wanted to "mate" her?

"Are you *sure* you're okay?" Chess said.

"Yeah. Sorry; I'm a little brain-dead. I didn't sleep well last night." Her plan for Chess was exactly the same as for her mother. Tell her everything—in a little while. When she was less upset about it.

Chess was putting an arm around her, steering skillfully with the other. "Hey, we've got to get you in shape, kid. I mean, first it's your birthday, then graduation. Isn't that psychologist doing anything to help?"

Hannah muttered, "Maybe too much."

That night, she was restless again. The school day had passed uneventfully. Hannah and her mother had had dinner peacefully. But after her mother went out to a meeting with some local rockhounds, Hannah found herself wandering around the house, too wound up to read or watch TV, too distracted to go anywhere.

Maybe I need some air, she thought—and then she caught herself and gave a self-mocking grin.

Sure. Air. When what you're *really* thinking is that he just might be out there. Admit it.

She admitted it. Not that she thought Thierry was very likely to be hanging around her backyard, considering what she'd said to him.

And why should you *want* to talk to him? she demanded of herself. He may not be completely and totally and pointlessly evil, but he's still no boy scout.

But she couldn't shake a vague feeling of wanting to go outside. At last she went out on the porch, telling herself that she'd spend five minutes here and then go back inside.

It was another beautiful night, but Hannah couldn't enjoy it. Everything reminded her too much of him. She could feel herself softening toward him, weakening. He had looked so stricken, so devastated, when she told him to go away. . . .

"Am I interrupting?"

Hannah started. She wheeled toward the voice.

Standing on the other side of the porch was a tall girl. She looked a year or so older than Hannah, and she had long hair, *very* long hair, so black that it seemed to reflect moonlight like a raven's wing. She was extraordinarily beautiful—and Hannah recognized her.

She's the one from my vision. That flash of a girl telling me that Thierry was cunning. She's the one who warned me about him.

And she's the figure I saw behind Chess's car this morning. She must have been watching me then.

"I'm sorry if I scared you," the girl said now, smiling. "You looked so far away, and I didn't mean to startle you. But I'd really like to talk to you if you have a few minutes."

"I . . ." Hannah felt strangely tongue-tied. Something about the girl made her uncomfortable, in a way that went beyond the dreamlike weirdness of recognizing somebody she'd never seen in her present life.

But she's your friend, she told herself. She's helped you in the past; she probably wants to help you again now. You should be grateful to her.

"Sure," Hannah said. "We can talk." She added somewhat awkwardly, "I remember you."

"Wonderful. Do you really? That makes everything so much easier."

Hannah nodded. And told herself again that this girl was her friend, and nobody to be hostile to or wary of.

"Well . . ." The girl glanced around the porch, where there was clearly no place to sit. "Ah . . ."

Hannah was embarrassed, as if the girl had asked, "Do

you entertain all your visitors outside?" She turned around and opened the back door. "Come on in. We can sit down."

"Thank you," the girl said and smiled.

In the bright fluorescent lights of the kitchen, she was even more beautiful. Hauntingly beautiful. Exquisite features, skin like silk. Lips that made Hannah think of adjectives like full and ripe. And eyes that were like nothing Hannah had ever seen before.

They were large, almond-shaped, heavy-lashed, and luminous. But it wasn't just that. Every time Hannah looked, they seemed to be a different color. They changed from honey to mahogany to jungle-leaf green to larkspur purple to misty blue. It was amazing.

"If you remember me, then you must know what I'm here about," the girl said. She rested an elbow on the kitchen table and propped her chin on her fist.

Hannah said one word. "Thierry."

"Yes. From the way you say that, maybe you don't need my advice after all." The girl had an extraordinary voice as well; low and pleasant, with a faint husky throb in it.

Hannah lifted her shoulders. "Well, there's still a lot I don't know about him—but I don't need anybody to tell me that he's dangerous. And I've already told him to go away."

"Have you really? How remarkably brave of you."

Hannah blinked. She hadn't thought of it as being so brave.

"I mean, you do realize how powerful he is? He's a Lord

of the Night World, the head of all the made vampires. He could"—the girl snapped her fingers—"call out a hundred little vampires and werewolves. Not to mention his connection with the witches in Las Vegas."

"What are you trying to say? That I *shouldn't* have told him to go away? I don't care how many monsters he can call out," Hannah said sharply.

"No. Of course you don't. Like I said, you're brave." The girl regarded her with eyes the deep purple of bittersweet nightshade. "I just want you to realize what he's capable of. He could have this whole county wiped out. He can be very cruel and very childish—if he doesn't get what he wants he'll simply go into a rage."

"And does he do that a lot—go into rages?"

"All the time, unfortunately."

I don't believe you.

The thought came to Hannah suddenly. She didn't know *where* it came from, but she couldn't ignore it. There was something about this girl that bothered her, something that felt like a greasy stone held between the fingers. That felt like a lie.

"Who are you?" she said directly. When the girl's eyes— now burnt sienna—lifted to hers this time, she held them. "I mean, why are you so interested in me? Why are you even *here*, in Montana, where I am? Is it just a coincidence?"

"Of course not. I came because I knew that he was about to find you again. I'm interested in you because—well, I've known Thierry since his childhood, before he became a vampire, and I feel a certain obligation to stop him." She smiled, meeting Hannah's steady gaze easily. "And my name . . . is Maya."

She said the last words slowly, and she seemed to be watching Hannah for a reaction. But the name didn't mean anything to Hannah. And Hannah simply couldn't figure out whether this girl called Maya was lying or not.

"I know you've warned me about Thierry before," Hannah said, trying to gather her thoughts. "But I don't remember anything about it except you telling me. I don't even know *what* you are—I mean, are you somebody who's been reincarnated like me? Or are you . . . ?" She left the question open-ended. As a matter of fact, she knew Maya wasn't human; no human was so eerily beautiful or supernaturally graceful. If Maya claimed she *was*, Hannah would know for sure it was a deception.

"I'm a vampire," Maya said calmly and without hesitation. "I lived with Thierry's tribe in the days when you lived with the Three Rivers clan. In fact, I'm the one who actually made him into a vampire. I shouldn't have done it; I should have realized he was one of those people who couldn't handle it. But I didn't know he'd go crazy and become . . . what he is." She looked off into the distance. "I suppose that's why I feel responsible for him," she finished softly. Then she looked back at Hannah. "Any other questions?"

"Hundreds," Hannah said. "About the Night World, and about what's happened to me in past lives—"

"And I'm afraid I'm not going to be able to answer most of them. There are rules against talking about the Night World— and anyway, it's safer for you not to know. As for your past lives, well, you don't really *want* to know what he's done to you each time, do you? It's too gruesome." She leaned forward, looking at Hannah earnestly. "What you should do now is put the past behind you and forget about all this. Try to have a happy future."

It was exactly what Hannah had decided to do earlier. So why did she feel like bristling now? She weighed different responses and finally said, "If he wants to kill me so much, why didn't he just do it last night? Instead of talking to me."

"Oh, my dear child." The tone was slightly patronizing, but seemed genuinely pitying. "He wants you to *love* him first, and then he kills you. I know, it's sick, it's twisted, but it's the way he is. He seems to think it has to be that way, since it was that way the first time. He's obsessed."

Hannah was silent. Nothing inside her stood up to say that this was a lie. And the idea that Thierry was obsessed certainly rang true. At last she said slowly, "Thank you for coming to warn me. I do appreciate it."

"No, you don't," Maya said. "I wouldn't either if someone came to tell me things I didn't want to hear. But maybe some-day you *will* thank me." She stood. "I hope we won't have to meet again."

Hannah walked her to the back door and let her out.

On the porch, Maya turned. "He really is insane, you know," she said. "You'll probably begin to have doubts again. But he's obsessive and unstable, just like any stalker; and he's really capable of anything. Don't be fooled."

"I don't think I'm ever going to see him again," Hannah said, unreasonably annoyed. "So it's going to be kind of hard to fool me."

Maya smiled, nodded, then did the disappearing act. Just as Thierry had, she turned and simply melted into the night.

Hannah stared out into the darkness for a minute or so. Then she went back into the kitchen and called Paul Winfield's number.

She got his answering machine. "Hi, this is Hannah, and I got your message about making another appointment. I was wondering if we could maybe do it tomorrow—or anyway some time over the weekend. And . . ." She hesitated, wondering if it was something she should say in person, then shrugged. Might as well give him time to prepare. "And I'd like to do another regression. There are some things I want to figure out."

She felt better after she hung up. One way or another, she would get at the truth.

She headed into her bedroom with a faint, grim smile.

And stopped dead on the threshold.

Thierry was sitting on her bed.

For a moment Hannah stood frozen. Then she said sharply, "What are you doing here?" At the same time, she glanced around the room to see how he had gotten in. The windows were shut and only opened from inside.

He must have walked in while I was in the kitchen talking with Maya.

"I had to see you," Thierry said. He looked—strange. His dark eyes seemed hot somehow, as if he were burning inside. His face was tense and grim.

"I told you to keep away from me." Hannah kept fear out of her voice—but she was scared. There was a sort of electricity in the air, but it wasn't a good electricity. It was purely dangerous.

"I know you did, and I tried. But I can't stay away, Hannah. I just can't. It makes me . . . crazy."

And with that, he stood up.

Hannah's heart seemed to jump into her throat and stay there, pounding hard. She fought to keep her face calm.

He's fast, a little voice in her head seemed to say, and with relief she recognized the dark wind voice, the cool voice of reason. *There's no point in running from him, because he can catch you in a second.*

"You have to understand," Thierry was saying. "Please try to understand. I *need* you. We were meant to be together. Without you, I'm nothing."

He took a step toward her. His eyes were black and fathomless, and Hannah could almost feel their heat. Obsessed, yes, she thought. Maya was right. He may put on a good front, but underneath he's just plain crazy. Like any stalker.

"Say you understand," Thierry said. He reached a pleading hand toward her.

"I understand," Hannah said grimly. "And I still want you to go away."

"I can't. I have to make sure we'll be together, the way we were meant to be. And there's only one way to do that."

There was something different about his mouth. Two delicate fangs were protruding, indenting his lower lip.

Hannah felt a cold fist close over her heart.

"You have to join the Night World, Hannah. You have to become like me. I promise you, once it's over, you'll be happy."

"Happy?" A wave of sickening revulsion swept over Hannah. "As a monster like you? I was *happy* before you ever showed up. I'd be happy if you'd just keep out of my life forever. I—"

Stop talking! The cool wind voice was screaming at her, but Hannah was too overwrought to listen.

"You're disgusting. I *hate* you. And nothing can ever make me love you ag—"

She didn't get to finish. In one swift movement, he was in front of her. And then he grabbed her.

CHAPTER 9

"Y ou'll change your mind," Thierry said.

An instant later everything was chaos. Thierry had one hand in her hair, twisting her head to the side, exposing her neck. His other arm was keeping both her arms trapped against her body. Hannah was twisting, struggling—and it wasn't doing any good. He was unbelievably strong.

She felt the warmth of breath on her neck . . . and then the sharpness of teeth.

"Don't fight." Thierry's muffled voice came to her. "You'll only make it hurt worse."

Hannah fought. And it did hurt. The pain of having blood drawn out against her will was like nothing she'd ever felt. It was as if her soul was being pulled out of her body, a pain that radiated down her neck and through her left shoulder and arm. It turned her vision gray and made her feel light-headed.

"I—*hate*—you," she got out. She tried to reach for him with her mind, to see if she could hurt him that way . . . but it was like running up against an obsidian wall. She could feel nothing of Thierry in the contact, just smooth black hardness.

Forget about that, the cool wind voice said. And don't faint; you've got to stay conscious. Think about your room. You need wood; you need a weapon. Where . . . ?

The desk.

Even as she thought it, Thierry's grip on her was shifting. He was forcing her to turn so she faced away from him, still holding her in an iron grip with one arm. She had no idea what he was doing with the other arm until he spoke again.

"I have to give you back something for what I took."

And then the other arm was in front of Hannah, wrist pressing to her mouth. She still didn't really understand—she was dazed with pain and loss of blood—until she felt warm liquid trickling into her mouth and tasted a strange exotic taste.

Oh, God—*no*. It's his *blood*. You're drinking vampire blood.

She tried not to swallow, but the liquid kept flowing in, choking her. It didn't taste at all like blood. It was rich and wild and burned slightly—and she could almost feel it changing her.

You've got to stop this, the cool wind voice told her. *Now.*

With a violent wrench that almost dislocated her shoulder, Hannah got one arm free. Then she started to fight hard, not because she wanted to get away, but because she wanted to keep Thierry occupied in holding her. While they were struggling, she surreptitiously reached out with her free hand.

I can't feel it. She threw her body back and forth, trying to get Thierry to move closer to the desk. Just a little farther . . . there. There!

Her fingers were on her desk. She stomped on Thierry's foot to keep him distracted. She heard a snarl of pain and Thierry shook her, but her fingers kept groping across the desk until they found something smooth and long, with a pointed graphite end.

A pencil.

Hannah curled her fingers, gathering the pencil into her fist. She was gasping with effort, which meant more of the strange blood was flowing into her mouth.

Now *think*. Visualize his hand. Picture the pencil going right in, all the way through. And now *strike*.

Hannah brought the pencil up with all her strength, driving it into the back of Thierry's hand.

She heard a yelp of pain and outrage—and at the same instant she felt a stab of pain herself. She'd driven the pencil all the way through his hand and jabbed her own cheek.

She didn't spend time worrying about it. The iron grip on her had loosened. She slammed a foot into Thierry's shin and spun away as he jerked back.

The desk! You need another weapon!

Even as the voice was telling her, Hannah was reaching for her desk, gathering a random handful of pens and pencils. Thank God for her habit of losing pencils, which was the reason she had to keep so many. As soon as she had them, she twisted to dart across the room, getting her back to a wall. She faced Thierry, panting.

"This next one goes right into your heart," she told him, pulling one pencil out of the handful and holding it in her fist. Her voice was soft and ragged, but absolutely deadly in its conviction.

"You hurt me!" Thierry had pulled the pencil out and was staring at the wound. His face was contorted, his eyes blazing with animal pain and fury. He looked like a stranger.

"Right," Hannah said, panting. "And if you come close to me again, I'll kill you. That's a promise. Now get the *hell* out of my house and out of my life!"

Thierry stared back and forth from her to his hand. Then he snarled—really snarled, his upper lip lifting, his teeth bared. Hannah had never seen a human face look so bestial.

"You'll be sorry," he said, like a child in a temper tantrum. "And if you tell anybody about this, I'll kill them. I will. It's Night World law."

Then he did the fade-out thing. Hannah blinked and he wasn't there. He must have backed up down the hall, but she didn't hear a door open or close.

It was several minutes before she could loosen her grip on

her pencil or step away from the wall. When she could, it was to stumble toward the phone. She pressed the speed dial for Chess's number.

Busy.

Hannah dropped the phone. She was swaying on her feet, feeling sick and giddy, but she headed for the dining room. There, keeping one of the windows shut, was a wooden dowel, the remnant of some long-past safety craze of her mother's. Hannah broke it over her knee and carried one splinter-ended piece with her to the garage.

The dusty old Ford was parked there, the one her father had driven before he died. Hannah found the keys and started for Chess's house. She could think of only one thing: she didn't want to be alone.

Gray spots danced in front of her eyes as she drove. She kept imagining things rushing at her from the prairie.

Stay awake. Just stay awake, she told herself, biting her lip hard enough to draw blood.

There! There's the house up ahead. You can see the light. All you have to do is get there.

She stepped on the accelerator. And then everything went gray.

Thierry looked around the resort lobby, then glanced at his watch. He'd been doing that every five minutes for about the last twelve hours, and his nerves were starting to fray.

He didn't like leaving Hannah alone. Of course, the ring would protect her when she was away from the house, and the amulet he'd buried in her backyard would protect the house itself. It was a strong amulet, made for him by Grandma Harman, the oldest and most powerful witch in the world, the Crone of the Inner Circle. It set wards around the house, so that no Night Person could enter without a direct invitation from somebody who lived inside.

He still didn't like leaving Hannah alone.

Only a little while longer, he told himself. It had taken him most of last night and all of today to call in enough of his own people to set up a plan for watching over Hannah.

She'd told him to go away, and he had. Her word was law to him. But that didn't mean he couldn't have her guarded. She need never realize that there were Night People around her, watching and waiting in the shadows—and ready to fight to the death if any danger appeared.

Lupe had been right. He couldn't deal with this alone. And now he was going to have to rely on other people to keep Hannah safe.

Thierry looked at his watch again. It was nine o'clock at night, and he was almost tempted to give up on Circe. But only a witch of her power could set up the kind of heavy-duty wards that would protect Hannah wherever she went in Amador County.

He kept waiting. As he did, he stared at a gun rack on the wall and tried to keep his brain turned off. It didn't work.

Ever since he'd awoken Hannah from her hypnotic trance, he'd been trying very hard not to think about the old days. But now, he found himself being irresistibly drawn back—not only thinking about them, but reliving them. Traveling back in his mind to the stupid young man he had been. . . .

He hadn't been the first vampire. He didn't have that distinction.

He had only been the second.

He'd grown up in the tribe of Maya and Hellewise. *The* Maya and Hellewise, the twin daughters of Hecate Witch Queen. The Maya and Hellewise who would go down as the two greatest figures in Night World history; Hellewise Hearth-Woman as the ancestress of the Harman family, the most famous of the living witches, and Maya as the ancestress of both the lamia and the made vampires.

But of course he knew nothing about that at the time.

All he knew was that they were both pretty girls. Beautiful. Hellewise had long yellow hair and deep brown eyes. Maya had long black hair and eyes that glittered in different colors like the changing lights in a glacier. He liked both sisters very much.

Maybe that was his downfall.

He'd been a very ordinary fellow, with a good throwing arm, a delicate touch in carving ivory, and a vague longing to see the world. He'd taken it for granted that his tribe was special, that they could influence the weather and summon animals from the forest. They were the witch people, they'd been granted special powers, and that was all. It wasn't anything to worry about.

And, like everyone else, he knew that Maya was doing experiments in the forest, using her powers to try and become immortal. But that didn't worry him particularly either. . . .

I was very young and very, very stupid, Thierry thought.

That had been the real downfall of the tribe. Maya's desire to become immortal. Because she'd been willing to pay any price for it, even to the point of becoming a monster and leaving a curse on all her descendants. Maybe if Thierry and the other witch people had realized that, they could have stopped her before it happened.

Because Maya had finally found the right spell to achieve immortality. The problem was that to do it, she had to steal the babies of the tribe. All four of them. She took them out to the forest, did the spell, and drank their blood. Thierry and the rest of the tribe found the four little bled-out bodies later.

Hellewise had cried all night. Thierry, who couldn't understand how the pretty girl he liked could have done something so awful, cried, too. Maya herself had disappeared completely.

But a few nights later she came to Thierry. He was keeping watch outside the cave when she appeared silently beside him.

She had changed.

She wasn't the pretty girl he knew anymore. She was stunningly, dazzlingly beautiful. But she was different. She moved with the grace of a nighttime predator, and her eyes reflected the firelight.

She was very pale, but that only made her more lovely. Her mouth, which had always been soft and inviting, seemed red as blood. And when she smiled at him, he saw her long pointed teeth.

"Hello, Theorn," she said—that was his name back then. "I want to make you immortal."

Thierry was scared out of his mind.

He had no idea what she'd become—some weird creature with unnatural teeth. But he knew he had no desire at all to be like her.

"I really think it's unfair, the way you go back and forth between me and Hellewise," she said casually, sitting down on the bare earth. "So I've decided to resolve the question. You're going to be mine, now and forever."

She reached out and took his hand. Her fingers were very slender and very cold—and unbelievably strong. Thierry couldn't pull away. He stared at his hand with his mouth open like the idiot he was.

This was the time he should have started yelling, thrashing, doing anything to attract attention and get away. But Maya seemed to hold him with her eyes like a snake holding a bird. She was unnatural and evil . . . but she was so beautiful.

It was the first and the last time that Thierry would be fascinated by the beauty of pure evil—but it was enough. He was doomed from that moment. He'd doomed himself.

An instant of hesitation. He would pay for it for unimaginable years in the future.

"It's not so bad," Maya was saying, still fixing him with her terrible and lovely eyes. "There are a few things I had to figure out—a few things I didn't expect. I thought drinking the blood of the babies would be the end of it, but no."

Thierry felt sick.

"I've got these teeth for a reason, apparently. It seems I have to drink the blood of a mortal creature every day, or I die. It's inconvenient, but I can live with it."

Thierry whispered something beginning with, "Oh, Hecate, Dark Mother—"

"Now, stop that!" Maya made a sharp gesture. "No praying, please, and especially not to that old harridan. I'm not a witch anymore. I'm something completely new—I suppose I should think of a name for myself. Night-hunter . . . blood-drinker . . . I don't know, the possibilities are endless. I'm going to start a new race, Theorn. We'll be better than the witches, stronger, faster—and we'll live forever. We'll never die, so we'll rule everyone. And you're going to be my first convert."

"No," Thierry said. He still thought he had a choice.

"Yes. I'm going to have a baby—not with you, I'm afraid; I don't think you'll be able to—and the baby will have my blood. And I'm going to give my blood to other people the way

I'll give it to you now. Someday there won't be anyone in the world who won't have my blood. It's a nice thought, isn't it?" She rested her chin on a fist and her eyes glittered.

"Hellewise will stop you," Thierry said flatly.

"My sister? No, I don't think so. Especially not since I'll have you to help me. She likes you, you know. It will be hard for her to kill somebody she likes so much."

"She won't have to. *I'll* kill you," Thierry snarled.

Maya laughed out loud.

"You? *You?* Don't you know yourself yet? You're not a killer—you don't have the guts for it. That will change, of course, after I give you my blood. But you won't want to kill me then. You'll join me—and be happy. You'll see." She dusted off her hands as if a difficult negotiation had been accomplished and terms had been reached. "Now. Let's do it."

He was strong. He had that good throwing arm—he was dead accurate with a spear or a killing stick. But she was so much stronger that she could handle him like a baby. The first thing she did was clamp a hand across his mouth—because by this time it had occurred even to stupid Thierry that he was in very bad trouble, and that he needed help.

There was no sound of a struggle as she dragged him off into the bushes.

"I'm afraid this is going to hurt," she said. She was lying on top of him, her eyes glittering into his. She was excited. "At least, all the animals I've caught seem to have found it very unpleasant. But it's for your own good."

Then she ripped his throat out.

That was what it felt like. And that was when he realized what those long canine teeth were for. Like any lynx or cave lion or wolf, she needed teeth to tear.

Through the black waves of shock and pain, he heard her drinking.

It lasted a long time. But finally, mercifully, he realized that he was dying. He took comfort in the thought that the horror would soon be over.

He couldn't have been more wrong. The horror was just beginning.

When Maya lifted her head, her mouth was scarlet with his blood. Dripping. She wasn't beautiful any longer, she was simply fiendish.

"Now," she said. "I'm going to give you something that will make it all better."

She pulled back and placed a fire-hardened splinter of wood at her own throat. She smiled at him. Maya had always been physically brave. And then, with a gesture almost of ecstasy, she plunged the splinter in, sending blood spurting and spilling.

Then she fell on top of him again.

He didn't mean to swallow the blood that filled his mouth. But everything was so gray and unreal—and he still had enough survival reflex left to not want to drown in it. The warm, strange-tasting liquid went down his throat. It burned like fermented-berry wine.

After she made him drink, he realized to his relief that he was still dying. He didn't know that he wasn't going to stay dead. He felt her carrying him farther into the forest—he was completely limp now and didn't put up any resistance—and then everything went black.

When he woke up, he'd been buried.

He clawed himself up out of the shallow grave and found himself looking into the astonished face of his brother Conlan. The tribe had buried him in the traditional way—in the soft dirt at the back of the cave.

In the minute before his brother could yell in surprise, Thierry was at his throat.

It was animal instinct. A thirst inside of him like nothing he had ever known. A pain that was like being underwater—being strangled—gasping for air. It made him desperate, made him insane. He didn't think at all.

He simply tried, mindlessly, to tear at his brother's throat.

What stopped him was someone calling his name. Calling it over and over, in great pain. When he looked around, he saw Hellewise, her brown eyes huge and spilling with tears, her mouth trembling.

The expression on her face would haunt him forever.

He ran out of the cave and kept running. Behind him, just faintly, he could hear Hellewise's voice, "Theorn, I'll stop her. I swear to you, I'll stop her."

He realized later that it was all Hellewise could offer him. She knew that his curse was permanent. What he was now, he would be forever.

There wasn't a name for it then, but he was the first made vampire. Maya, who would have a son just as she promised, was the first of the lamia, the family vampires who could grow up and have children. And her son, Red Fern, would be the ancestor of the Redfern family, the most powerful lamia family in the Night World.

Thierry didn't know any of that as he ran. He only knew he had to get away from people, or he would hurt them.

Maya caught up with him while he was frantically trying to quench his thirst by drinking from a stream.

"You're going to make yourself sick," she said, inspecting him critically. "You can't drink that. It's blood you need."

Thierry jumped up, shaking with fury and hatred and weakness all mixed together. "What about *yours*?" he snarled.

Maya laughed. "How sweet. But it won't do. You need the blood of living creatures." She wasn't at all afraid of him, and he remembered how strong she had been. He was no match for her.

He turned and began to stumble off.

Maya called after him, "You can't do it, you know. You can't get away from me. I've *chosen* you, Theorn. You're mine, now and forever. And in the end you'll realize that and join me."

Thierry kept going. He could hear her laughing as he went.

He lived on the steppes for several weeks, wandering across the high windswept grasslands. He was more an animal than anything resembling a person. The thirst inside him made him desperate—until he stumbled over a rabbit. The next instant he found that he was holding it, biting into its throat. His teeth were like Maya's now—long, sensitive, and perfect for tearing or puncturing. And she was right, only the blood of a living creature could help the burning, suffocating feeling inside him.

He didn't catch food very often. Every time he drank, it reminded him of what he was.

He was starving when he finally came to the Three Rivers.

He didn't see the little girl out picking spring greens until he was on top of her. He burst out of a pile of brush, panting with thirst like a wounded deer—and there she was, looking up at him. And then everything went dark for a while.

When he came to himself, he stopped drinking. He needed the food, he would die in terrible agony without it—but he dropped the girl and ran. Hana's people found him a little while later.

And they did exactly what he'd expected any tribe to

do—they saw that he was an abomination and brandished spears at him. He expected them to kill him at any minute. He didn't realize yet—and neither did they—that a creature like him took some killing.

And then he saw Hana.

CHAPTER 10

The first sight of her broke through his animal state and gave him enough mind to stand up like a man. She reminded him of Hellewise. She had that same look of tender courage, that same ageless wisdom in her eyes. Any woman could be pretty by virtue of regular features. But Hana was beautiful because her soul showed in her face.

Seeing her made him ashamed. Seeing her defend him, intercede on his behalf as she was so obviously doing, made him angry.

He resisted when she sneaked him out of the cave and tried to send him back into the world. Didn't she understand? It was best for him to die. As long as he was loose, no child, no woman, no man was safe. Even as he stood there in the moonlight with her, he was trembling with need. The bloodlust was trying to unbalance his mind, and it was all he could do not to grab *her* and bite into her soft throat.

When she offered him her throat, he almost cried. It wasn't a sacrifice to turn her down and walk away. It was the only right thing to do, the only thing he could do.

And then the hunters came.

His mind was unbalanced by the torture. It was that simple. Not that it was an excuse, there was no excuse for what followed. But during the endless time while Hana's clan burned and stabbed and beat him, he lost all contact with the person he thought of as himself. He became an animal, as mindless as the mob that was trying to kill him.

As an animal, he wanted two things: to survive and to strike out at the people who were hurting him. And there was a way to do both.

Throats. White throats, spurting dark blood. The image came to him slowly in his haze of pain. He didn't have to lie here and take this. He was wounded, but there was still a granite core of strength inside him. He could fight back, and his enemies would give him life.

The next time a spear jabbed at him, he grabbed it and pulled.

It belonged to the broad-shouldered hunter, the one who'd led the others to him. Thierry grabbed the man as he stumbled forward, wrestling him to the ground. And then, before anyone in the crowd had time to react, he darted for the hunter's throat, for the big vein that pulsed just under the skin.

It was all over in a minute. He was drinking deep, deep,

and gaining strength with every swallow. The clan of the Three Rivers was staring at him in paralyzed shock.

It felt good.

He tossed the dead man aside and reached for another.

When several hunters came at him at once, he knocked them apart and killed them, one, two, three. He was a very efficient killer. The blood made him supernaturally strong and fast, and the bloodlust gave him motivation. He was like a wolf set loose in a herd of antelope—except that for a long time nobody in the clan had the sense to run. They kept coming at him, trying to stop him, and he kept killing.

It was a slaughter. He killed them all.

He was drunk with blood and he gloried in it, in the animal simplicity of it, the power it gave him. Killing *was* glory. Killing to eat, killing for revenge. Destroying the people who hurt him. He didn't ever want to stop.

He was drinking the last drops from the veins of a young girl when he looked down and saw it was Hana.

Her clear gray eyes were wide open, but the light in them was beginning to go dark.

He'd killed her.

In one blinding instant he wasn't an animal anymore. He was a person. And he was looking down at the one person who had tried to help him, who had offered him her blood to keep him alive.

He raised his eyes and saw the devastation he'd left in

the cave. It wasn't just this girl. He'd murdered most of her tribe.

That was when he knew the truth. He was damned. Worse than Maya. He'd committed a crime so monstrous that he could never be forgiven, never be redeemed. He had joined evil in the end, just as Maya had promised he would.

No punishment could be too great for him—but then, no punishment would make the slightest difference anyway, not to these people or to the dying girl in his arms.

For just an instant some part of him pushed away at the feelings of guilt and horror. All right, you're evil, it said. You might as well go ahead and *be* evil. Enjoy it. Have no regrets. It's your nature, now. Give in.

Then the girl in his arms stirred.

She was still conscious, although barely. Her eyes were still open. She was looking up at him. . . .

In that moment, Thierry felt a shock that was different from anything he'd ever felt before.

In those large gray eyes, in the pupils that were hugely dilated as if to catch every last ray of light before death, he saw . . . himself.

Himself and the girl, walking together, hand in hand through the ages. Joined. Shifting scenes behind them, different places, different times. But always the two of them, tied with an invisible bond.

He *recognized* her. It was almost as if all those different ages had already happened, as if he were only remembering them. But he knew they were in the future. He was looking down the corridor of time, seeing what *should have been.*

She was his soulmate.

She was the one who was supposed to have walked with him through different lives, being born and loving and dying and being born again. They'd been born *for* each other, to help each other grow and blossom and discover and evolve. They should have had many lives together.

And none of it was going to happen. He was an immortal creature—how could he die and be born again? And she was dying *because* of him. He'd destroyed it all, everything. He'd killed his destiny.

In the enormity of it, he sat silent and stunned. He couldn't say, "I'm sorry." He couldn't say, "What have I done?" There was nothing that he could say that wasn't so trivial as to be demeaning to her. He simply sat and shook, looking down into her eyes. He had an endless feeling of falling.

And then Hana spoke.

I forgive you.

It was just a whisper, but he heard it in his mind, not with his ears. And he understood it, even though her language was different from his. Thierry reeled with the discovery that he could talk to her. Oh, Goddess, the chance at least to tell her how he would try to atone for this by spilling out his own blood. . . .

You can't forgive me. He could see that she understood his own hushed answer. He knew he didn't deserve forgiveness. But part of him wanted her to realize that he had never meant this to happen. *I wasn't always like this. I used to be a person—*

We don't have time for that, she told him. Her spirit seemed to be reaching toward him, drawing him into her, facing him in a still and separate place where only the two of them existed. He knew then that she had seen the same thing he had, the same corridor of time.

She was gentle, but so sad. *I don't want you to die. But I want you to promise me one thing.*

Anything.

I want you to promise me you'll never kill again.

It was easy to promise. He didn't plan to live . . . no, she didn't want him to die. But he couldn't live without her and he certainly couldn't live after what he'd done.

He'd worry about it later, about how to deal with the long gray stretch of future waiting for him. For now, he said, *I'll never kill again.*

She gave him just the faintest of smiles.

And then she died.

The gray eyes went fixed and dark. Unseeing. Her skin was ghostly white and her body was absolutely still. She seemed smaller all at once as her spirit left her.

Thierry cradled her, moaning like a wounded animal. He was crying. Shaking so hard he almost couldn't keep hold of her. Helpless, pierced by love that felt like a spear, he reached out to gently push her hair off her face. His thumb stroked her cheek—and left a trail of blood.

He stared at it in horror. The mark was like a blaze of red against her pale skin.

Even his love was deadly. His caress had branded her.

The few survivors of Hana's clan were on the move, surrounding Thierry, panting and gasping with their spears ready. They sensed that he was vulnerable now.

And he wouldn't have lifted a hand to stop them . . . except that he had made a promise to Hana. She wanted him alive to keep it.

So he left her there. He picked up her still, cooling body and carried it toward the nearest hunter. The man stared at him in fear and disbelief, but he finally dropped his spear to take the dead girl. And then Thierry walked out of the cave and into the merciless sunlight.

He headed for his home.

Maya caught up with him somewhere on the steppes, appearing out of the tall, ripping grass, "I told you how you'd end up. Now forget that washed-out blonde and start enjoying life with me."

Thierry didn't even look at her. The only thing he could imagine doing with Maya was killing her . . . and he couldn't do that.

"Don't walk away from me!" Maya wasn't laughing now.

She was furious. Her voice followed him as he kept going. "I *chose* you, Theorn! You're mine. You *can't* walk away from me!"

Thierry kept going, neither slower nor faster, letting her voice blend into the humming of the insects on the grassland. But her mental voice followed him.

I'll never let you get away. You'll always be mine, now and forever.

Thierry traveled fast, and in only a few days, he reached home and the person he'd come to see.

Hellewise looked up from her drying herbs and gasped.

"I'm not going to hurt you," he said. "I need your help."

What he wanted from her was a spell to sleep. He wanted to sleep until Hana was born again.

"It could be a long time," Hellewise said when he told her the whole story. "It sounds as if her soul has been damaged. It could be hundreds of years—even thousands."

Thierry didn't care.

"And you might die," Hellewise said, looking at him steadily with her deep, soft brown eyes. "And with what you've become—I don't think creatures like you are reborn. You would just . . . die."

Thierry simply nodded. He was only afraid of two things: that Maya would find him while he was asleep, and that he wouldn't know when to wake up.

"I can arrange the second," Hellewise said quietly. "You're

L. J. SMITH

linked anyway; your souls are one. When she's born again, voices from the Other Side will whisper to you."

Thierry himself figured out how to solve the first problem. He dug himself a grave. It was the only place where he could count on being safe and undisturbed.

Hellewise gave him an infusion of roots and bark and Thierry went to sleep.

He slept a long time.

He slept straight through the epic battle when Hellewise drove Maya and her son Red Fern out of the tribe and away from the witches. He slept through the origins of the Night World and thousands of years of human change. When he finally woke up, the world was a different place, with civilizations and cities. And he knew that somewhere Hana had been born in one of them.

He began to look.

He was a wanderer, a lost soul with no home and no people. But not a killer. He learned to take blood without killing, to find willing donors instead of hunting terrified prey.

He looked in every village he passed, learning about the new world surrounding him, surviving on very little, searching every face he saw. Lots of communities would have been glad to adopt him, this tall young man with dusty clothes and far-seeing eyes. But he only stayed long enough to make sure that Hana wasn't there.

When he did find her it was in Egypt, the Kingdom of the

Two Lands. She was sixteen. Her name was Ha-nahkt.

And Thierry would have recognized her anywhere, because she was still tall, still fair-haired and gray-eyed and beautiful.

Except for one thing.

Across her left cheek, where his fingers had smeared her own blood the night that he had killed her, was a red mark like a bruise. Like a stain on her perfect skin.

It was a sort of psychic brand, a physical reminder of what had happened in her last life. A permanent wound. And it was his fault.

Thierry was overcome with grief and shame. He saw that the other girl, Ket, the friend who had been with Hana in the last life, was with her again now. She had friends. Maybe it was best to leave her alone in this life, not even try to speak to her.

But he had forgotten about Maya.

Vampires don't die.

Life is strange sometimes. It was just as Thierry was thinking this that a figure walked into the lobby. Still half in his daydream of the past, he was expecting it to be Circe, so for a moment he was simply confused. Then his heart rate picked up and every muscle in his body tensed violently.

It was Maya.

He hadn't seen her for over a hundred years. The last time had been in Quebec, when Hannah had been named Annette.

And Maya had just killed her.

Thierry stood up.

She was as beautiful as ever. But to Thierry it was like the rainbow on oil scum. He hated her more than he had ever imagined he could hate anyone.

"So you found me," he said quietly. "I knew you'd show up eventually."

Maya smiled brilliantly. "I found *her* first."

Thierry went still.

"That amulet was a very good one. I had to wait around to catch her alone so she could invite me inside."

Thierry's heart lurched. He felt a physical wrench, as if something in him were actually trying to get out, trying desperately to get to Hannah—now.

How could he have been so stupid? She was too innocent; of course she would invite someone into her house. And she thought of Maya as a friend.

The ring should have offered at least a measure of protection from mind control—but only if Hannah had kept it on. Thierry realized now that she probably hadn't.

His voice a bare whisper, he said, "What did you do to her?"

"Oh, not much. Mostly it was just conversation. I mentioned that you were likely to get rough with her if things didn't go your way." Maya tilted her head, eyes on his face, looking for a reaction.

Thierry didn't give it to her. He just stood, watching her silently.

She hadn't changed in thousands of years. She *never* changed, never grew, never got tired. And she never gave up. He didn't think she was capable of it.

Sometimes he thought he should just tie himself to her at the waist and find a bottomless pit to jump into. Rid the world of its two oldest vampires and all the problems Maya caused.

But there was his promise to Hannah.

"It doesn't matter what you say to her," he said stonily. "You don't understand, Maya. This time is different. She remembers and—"

"And she hates you. I know. Poor baby." Maya made a mock-sympathetic face. Her eyes sparkled peacock blue.

Thierry gritted his teeth. "And I've come to a decision," he went on evenly. "The cycle has to be broken. And there *is* a way to do it."

"I know," Maya said before he could finish. "You can give her up. Give in to me—"

"Yes." This time he cut her off. And the look of astonishment that flared in her eyes was worth it. "At least, yes to the first part," he finished. "I'm giving her up."

"You're not. You can't."

"She's happy in this life. And she—doesn't want me." There. It had been hard to say, but he'd gotten it out. "She remembers everything—I don't know why, but she does. Maybe because she's so close to her original form. Maybe somehow the memories are closer to the surface. Or maybe it's the hypnosis. But in any case, she doesn't want me anymore."

Maya was watching him, fascinated, her eyes the violet of deep twilight, her lips parted. Suddenly, she looked beyond him and smiled secretly. "She remembers everything? You really think so?"

Thierry nodded. "All I've ever brought her is misery and pain. I guess she realizes that." He took a breath, then caught Maya's eyes again. "So I'm ending the cycle . . . now."

"You're going to walk away."

"And so are you. She's no threat to you anymore. If you want something from me, the only person to deal with is me. You can try any time you like in Vegas." He gazed at her levelly.

Maya threw back her head and let out ripples of musical laughter.

"Oh, why didn't you tell me before? You could have saved me some trouble . . . but on the other hand, her blood was very sweet. I wouldn't have missed—"

She broke off, then, because Thierry slammed her against the oak-paneled wall of the lobby.

In one instant, his control had disappeared. He was so angry that he couldn't speak out loud.

What did you do to her? What did you do? He shouted the words telepathically as his hands closed around Maya's throat.

Maya just smiled at him. She was the oldest vampire, and

the most powerful. In every vampire who came after her, her blood had been diluted, half as strong, a quarter as strong, an eighth. But she was the original and the purest. She wasn't afraid of anyone.

Me? I *didn't do anything,* she said, answering him the same way. *I'm afraid* you *were the one who attacked her. She seemed very unhappy about it; she even stabbed you with a pencil.* Maya lifted a hand and Thierry saw a neat dark hole puncturing it, faintly ringed with blood.

The power of illusion, he thought. Maya could appear as anyone and anything she wanted. She had talents that usually only belonged to werewolves and shapeshifters. And of course she was a witch.

She really has extraordinary spirit, Maya went on. *But she's all right—you didn't exchange as much blood as you'd planned. The pencil, you see.*

People were gathering behind Thierry, murmuring anxiously. They were about to interfere and ask him to please let go of the girl he was strangling.

He ignored them.

Listen to me, he told Maya, staring into her mocking golden eyes. *Listen, because I'm never going to say this again. If you touch Hannah again—ever—in any life—I will kill you.*

"I'll kill you," he whispered out loud, to emphasize it. "Believe me, Maya, I'll do it."

Then he let her go. He had to get to Hannah. Even a small

exchange of blood with a vampire could be dangerous, and Maya's blood was the most potent on earth. Worse, he'd already taken some of Hannah's blood last night. She could be critically weak now . . . or starting to change.

He wouldn't think about that.

You won't, you know. Maya's telepathic voice followed him as he made for the door. *You won't kill me. Not Thierry the compassionate, Thierry the good vampire, Thierry the saint of Circle Daybreak. You're not capable of it. You* can't *kill.*

Thierry stopped on the threshold and turned around. He stared directly into Maya's eyes.

"Try me."

Then he was outside, moving quickly through the night. Even so, Maya got the last word.

And, of course, there's your promise. . . .

CHAPTER 11

Hannah stirred.

She vaguely felt that something was wrong, something needed doing. Then she remembered. The car! She had to stay awake, had to keep the car on the road. . . .

Her eyes flew open.

She was already off the road. The Ford had gone roving over the open prairie, where there was almost nothing to hit except sagebrush and tumbleweeds. It had ended up with its front bumper against a prickly pear, bending the cactus at an impossible angle.

The night was very quiet. She looked around and found that she could see the light of Chess's house, behind her and to the left.

The engine was off. Hannah turned the key in the ignition, but only got a grinding sound.

Now what? Should I get out and walk?

She tried to concentrate on her body, to figure out how she felt. She ought to feel terrible—after all, she'd lost blood and swallowed who knew what kind of poison from Thierry's veins.

But instead she only felt strangely dizzy, slightly dreamy.

I can walk. I'm fine.

Holding on to her length of dowel, she got out of the car and started toward the light. She could hardly feel the rough ground and the bluestem grass under her feet.

She had gone about a hundred yards toward the light when she heard a wolf howl.

It was such a distinctive sound—and so incongruous. Hannah stopped in her tracks. For a wild moment she wondered if coyotes howled.

But that was ridiculous. It was a wolf, just like the wolves that had attacked her at Paul's. And she didn't have anything made of silver.

Just keep walking, she thought. She didn't need the cool wind voice to tell her that.

Even in her light-headed state, she was frightened. She'd seen the savagery of teeth and claws close up. And the part of her that was Hana of the Three Rivers had a gut-deep fear of wild animals that the civilized Hannah Snow could never begin to approach.

She gripped her stick in a clammy palm and kept walking grimly.

The howl sounded again, so close that Hannah jumped inside her skin. Her eyes darted, trying to pick objects out in the darkness. She felt as if she could see better than usual at night—could the vampire blood have done that? But even with her new vision, she couldn't spot anything moving. The world around her was deserted and eerily quiet.

And the stars were very far away. They blazed in the sky with a cold blue light as if to show how distant they were from human affairs.

I could die here and they'd go right on shining, Hannah thought. She felt very small and very unimportant—and very alone.

And then she heard a breath drawn behind her.

Funny. The wolf howls had been so loud, and this was so soft . . . and yet it was much more terrifying. It was close—intimate. A *personal* sound that told her she definitely wasn't alone.

Hannah whirled with her stick held ready. Her skin was crawling and she could feel a wash of acid from her stomach, but she meant to fight for her life. She was at one with the cool wind voice; her heart was dark and cold and steely.

A tall figure was standing there. Starlight reflected off pale blond hair.

Thierry.

Hannah leveled her stick.

"What's the matter? Come back for more?" she said, and

she was pleased to find her voice steady. Husky, but steady. She waved her stick at him to show what kind of "more" she meant.

"Are you all right?" Thierry said.

He looked—different from the last time she'd seen him. His expression was different. His dark eyes seemed pensive again, the sort of expression a star might have if it cared about anything that was going on underneath it. Infinitely remote, but infinitely sad, too.

"Why should you care?" A wave of dizziness went through her. She fought it off—and saw that he was stepping toward her, hand reaching out. She whipped the stick up to the exact level of his hand, an inch from his palm. She was impressed with herself for how fast she did it. Her body was moving the way it had with the werewolves, instinctively and smoothly.

I suppose I had a life as a warrior, she mused. I think that's where the cool wind voice comes from, just the way the crystal voice comes from Hana of the Three Rivers.

"I do care," Thierry said. His voice said he didn't expect her to believe it.

Hannah laughed. The combination of her dizziness and her body instinct was having an odd effect. She felt brashly, stupidly overconfident. Maybe this is what drunk feels like, she thought, her mind wandering again.

"Hannah—"

Hannah made the stick whistle in the air, stopping him

from coming any closer to her. "Are you *crazy?*" she said. There were tears in her eyes. "Do you think that you can just attack me and then come back and say 'I'm sorry' and it's all going to be okay? Well, it isn't. If there was ever anything between us, it's all over now. There is no second chance."

She could see his face tense. A muscle twitched in his tight jaw. But the strangest thing was that she could have sworn he had tears in his eyes, too.

It infuriated her. How dare he pretend to be hurt by her, after what he'd done?

"I hate you." She spat the words with a force that startled even her. "I don't need you. I don't want you. And I'm telling you for the third time, *keep the hell away from me.*"

He had opened his mouth as if he were about to say something, but when she got to "I don't need you," he suddenly shut it. When she finished, he looked away, across the short-grass prairie.

"And maybe that's best," he said almost inaudibly.

"For you to keep away?"

"For you to hate me." He looked at her again. Hannah had never seen eyes like that before. They were impossibly distant and shattered and still . . . like the peace after a war that killed everyone.

"Hannah, I came to tell you that I *am* going away," he went on. His voice was like his eyes, bloodless and quenched. "I'm going home. I won't bother you again. And you're right; you don't need me. You can live a long and happy life without me."

If he expected her to be impressed, she wasn't. She wouldn't believe words from him anymore.

"There's just one thing." He hesitated. "Before I go, would you let me look at you? At your neck. I want to make sure that"—another fleeting hesitation—"that I didn't hurt you when I attacked you."

Hannah laughed again, a short, sharp bark of a laugh. "How stupid do you think I am? I mean, *really.*" She laughed again and heard an edge of hysteria in it. "If you want to do something for me, you can turn around and *go.* Go away forever."

"I will." There was so much strain on his face. "I promise. I'm just worried about you getting indoors before you faint."

"I can take care of myself. I don't need any help from you." Hannah was feeling dizzier by the minute, but she tried not to let it show. "If you would just leave, I'll be fine."

In fact, she knew she wasn't going to be fine. The gray spots were swarming in front of her eyes again. She was going to pass out soon.

Then I'd better start for Chess's, she thought. It was insanity to turn her back on him, but it was worse insanity to stand here until she collapsed at his feet.

"I'm leaving now," she said, trying to sound clear and precise and unlike someone who was about to fall over unconscious. "And I don't want you to follow me."

She turned and started walking.

I will not faint, I will not faint, she told herself grimly. She swung her stick and tried to take deep breaths of the cool night air. But tufts of grass seemed to be trying to trip her up with every step and the entire landscape seemed to rock every time she looked up.

I . . . will . . . not . . . faint. She knew her life depended on it. The ground seemed rubbery now, as if her feet were sinking into it and then rebounding. And where was the light that marked Chess's house? It had somehow gotten over to the right of her. She corrected her course and stumbled on.

I will not faint. . . .

And then her legs simply melted. She didn't *have* legs. The rest of her fell slowly toward the ground. Hannah managed to break her fall with her arms. Then everything was still and dark.

She didn't go out completely. She was floating in darkness, feeling woozy even though she was lying down, when she sensed someone beside her.

No, she thought. Get the stick. He'll bite you; he'll kill you.

But she couldn't move. Her hand wouldn't obey her.

She felt a gentle hand brush her hair off her face.

No . . .

Then a touch on her neck. But it was only gentle fingers, running lightly over the skin where she'd been bitten tonight. They felt like a doctor's fingers, exploring to diagnose. She heard a sigh that sounded like relief, and then the fingers trailed away.

"You'll be all right." Thierry's voice came to her softly. She realized he didn't think she could hear him. He thought she was unconscious. "As long as you stay away from vampires for the next week."

Was that a threat? Hannah didn't understand. She braced herself for the piercing pain of teeth.

Then she felt him touch her again, just his fingertips brushing her face. The touch was so immeasurably gentle. So tender.

No, Hannah thought. She wanted to move, to kick him away. But she couldn't.

And those delicate fingers were moving on, tracing her features one by one. With the lightest of touches that sent helpless chills through her.

I hate you, Hannah thought.

The touch followed the curve of her eyebrow, trailed down her cheek to her birthmark. Hannah shivered inwardly. It sketched the line of her jaw, then moved to her lips.

The skin was so sensitive here. Thierry's fingers traced the outline of her lips, the join between upper and lower. The chills became a fluttering inside Hannah. Her heart swelled with love and longing.

I won't feel this way. I *hate* you. . . .

But a voice was whispering in her mind, a voice she hadn't heard in what seemed like a long time. A crystal voice, soft but ringing.

Feel him. Does this feel like that other one? Sense him. Does he smell the same, sound the same . . . ?

Hannah didn't know what to make of the words and didn't want to. She just wanted Thierry to stop.

The fingers brushed over her eyelashes, thumb stroking over the fragile skin of her eyelids as if to keep them shut. Then she felt him bend closer.

No, no, no. . . .

Warm lips touched her forehead. Again, just the barest touch. Then they were gone.

"Goodbye, Hannah," Thierry whispered.

Hannah felt herself lifted. She was being carried in strong gentle arms, moving swiftly and smoothly.

It was harder for her to stay conscious than it had been before. She had a strange feeling of tranquillity, of security. But she fought to open her eyes just a crack.

She wanted to see his hands. She didn't think there had been enough time for the pencil wound to heal completely.

If the pencil wound was there.

But her eyes wouldn't open—not until she felt herself being lowered and placed on solid ground. Then she managed to lift heavy eyelids and dart a glance at his hands.

There were no marks.

The knowledge burned through her—but she didn't have any strength left. She felt her eyes lapsing shut again. Dimly, very far away, she could hear the faint echo of a doorbell.

Then a soft voice in her head. *You don't have to be afraid anymore. I'm going away—and so is* she.

Don't go. Wait. I have to talk to you. I have to ask you . . .

But she could feel cold air all around her and she knew he was gone.

A moment later she heard the door open, and the sound of Chess's mother gasping. She was on the Clovises' doorstep. People were shaking her, talking to her.

Hannah wasn't interested in any of it. She let the darkness take her.

It was when she let go completely that she began to dream. She was Hana of the Three Rivers and she was seeing the end of her own life.

She saw the bruised and bloody figure of Thierry rising up to kill his torturers. She felt it as her turn came. She looked up and saw his savage face, saw the animal light in his eyes. She felt her life flow away.

Then she saw the end of the story. The glimpse of the corridor through time, the recognition of her soulmate. The forgiveness and the promise.

And then just shadows. But Hannah slept peacefully in the shadows until morning, unafraid.

The first thing Hannah saw when she woke up was a pair of glowing green cat-eyes looking down at her.

"How do you feel?" Chess asked.

She was lying in Chess's bed. Sunlight was streaming in the window.

"I . . . can't tell yet," Hannah said. Disjointed images were floating in her head, not quite forming a whole picture.

"We found you last night," Chess said. "You ran your dad's car off the road, but you managed to make it here before you collapsed."

"Oh . . . yeah. I remember." She *did* remember; the pieces of the puzzle suddenly clicked together. Maya. Thierry. The attack. The car. Thierry again. And finally her dream. Her own voice saying, "I forgive you."

And now he was gone. He'd gone home, wherever home was. She had never felt so confused.

"Hannah, what *happened*? Are you sick? We didn't know whether to take you to a hospital last night or what. But you didn't have a fever and you seemed to be breathing fine—so my mom said you could just sleep a while."

"I'm not sick." This was the time to tell Chess everything. After all, that was the reason she'd been running to Chess in the first place last night.

But now . . . now in the bright morning light, she didn't want to tell Chess. It wasn't just that it might put Chess in danger, either from Thierry or the Night World in general. It was that Hannah didn't *need* to talk about it; she could cope on her own. It wasn't Chess's problem.

And I don't even know the truth yet, Hannah thought. But *that* is going to change.

"Hannah, are you even listening to me?"

"Yeah. I'm sorry. And I'm okay; I felt kind of dizzy last night, but now I'm better. Can I use your phone?"

"Can you *what*?"

"I have to call Paul—you know, the psychologist. I need to see him, fast."

She jumped up, steadied herself against a brief wave of giddiness, and walked past Chess, who was watching her in bewilderment.

"No," Paul said. "No, it's absolutely out of the question." He waved his hands, then patted his pockets nervously, coming up empty.

"Paul, please. I *have* to do this. And if you won't help me, I'll try it on my own. I think self-hypnosis should work. I've been doing a pretty good job of dreaming the past lately, anyway."

"It's . . . too . . . dangerous." Paul said each word separately, then sank into his chair, hands at his temples. "Don't you *remember* what happened the last time?"

Hannah felt sorry for him. But she said ruthlessly, "If I do it on my own, it may be even more dangerous. Right? At least if you hypnotize me you can be there to wake me up. You can throw a glass of water in my face again."

He looked up sharply. "Oh, yeah? And what if it doesn't work this time?"

Hannah dropped her eyes. Then she raised them and looked at Paul directly. "I don't know," she admitted quietly. "But I've still got to try. I have to know the truth. If I don't, I really think I may go insane." She didn't say it melodramatically. It was a simple statement of fact.

Paul groaned. Then he grabbed a pen and started chewing on it, glancing around the room. "What is it that you would want to know? Just presuming that I agreed to help you." His voice sounded squashed.

Hannah felt a surge of relief. "I want to know about this woman who keeps warning me," she said. "Her name is Maya. And I want to know how I die in my other lives."

"Oh, terrific. That sounds like fun."

"I *have* to do it." She took a deep breath. She wouldn't let herself look away from him, even though she could feel the warmth as her eyes filled. "Look, I know you don't understand. And I can't explain to you how important it is to me. But it is . . . important."

There was a silence, then Paul said, "All right. All right. But only because I think it's safer for you to be with somebody."

Hannah whispered, "Thank you."

Then she blinked and unfolded a piece of paper. "I wrote down some questions for you to ask me."

"Great. Wonderful. I'm sure you'll be getting your degree in psychology soon." But he took the paper.

Hannah walked over to the couch and got herself settled. She shut her eyes, telling her muscles to relax.

"Okay," Paul said. His voice was very slightly unsteady, but Hannah could tell he was trying to make it soothing. "I want you to imagine a beautiful violet light . . ."

CHAPTER 12

She was sixteen and her name was Ha-nahkt. She was a virgin priestess dedicated to the goddess Isis.

She was wearing a fine linen shift that fell from her waist to her ankles. Above the waist, she wore nothing except a deep silver collar strung with beads of amethyst, carnelian, turquoise, and lapis lazuli. There were two silver bracelets on her upper arms and two on her wrists.

Morning was her favorite time.

This morning she carefully placed her offering in front of the statue of Isis. Lotus blossoms, small cakes, and beer. Then, facing south, she began the chant to wake the goddess up.

> *"Awaken, Isis, Mother of the Stars,*
> *Great of Magic,*
> *Mistress of all the World,*
> *Sovereign of her father,*

Mightier than the gods,
Lady of the Waters of Life,
Powerful of Heart,
Isis of the Ten Thousand Names . . ."

A step sounded behind her and she broke off short, feeling startled and annoyed.

"I'm sorry. Did I disturb you?"

It was a woman, a beautiful woman with long black hair.

"You're not allowed in here," Ha-nahkt said sharply. "Only priests and priestesses . . ." Her voice trailed off as she looked at the woman more closely. Maybe she *is* a priestess, she thought. There's something in her face. . . .

"I just want to talk to you," the woman said. Her voice was husky and persuasive, almost mesmerizing. "It's very important." She smiled and Ha-nahkt felt hairs stir at the back of her neck.

If she's a priestess, I bet she's a priestess of Set. Set was the most evil of all the gods—and one of the most powerful. Ha-nahkt could sense power in this woman, no question about that. But evil? She wasn't sure.

"My name is Maya. And what I have to tell you may save your life."

Ha-nahkt stood still. Part of her wanted to run from Maya, to go and get her best friend Khet-hetepes. Or, better yet, one of the senior priestesses. But another part of her was curious.

"I really shouldn't stop in the middle of the chant," she began.

"It's about the stranger."

Ha-nahkt lost her breath.

There was a long moment of silence, and then she said, "I don't know what you're talking about." She could hear the shake in her own voice.

"Oh, yes, you do. The stranger. Tall, blond, handsome . . . and with such sad dark eyes. The one you've been meeting on the sly."

Ha-nahkt could feel the shaking take over her whole body. She was a priestess, sworn to the goddess. If anyone found she'd been meeting a man. . . .

"Oh, don't worry, little one," Maya said and laughed. "I'm not here to turn you in. Just the opposite, in fact. I want to help you."

"We haven't done anything," Ha-nahkt faltered. "Just kissed. He says he doesn't want me to leave the temple. He isn't going to stay long. He says he saw me, and he just had to speak to me."

"And no wonder," Maya said in a cooing tone. She touched Ha-nahkt's hair lightly and Ha-nahkt moved instinctively away. "You're such a pretty girl. Such unusual coloring for this part of the world. I suppose you think you love him."

"I *do* love him," Ha-nahkt blurted before she could stop herself. Then she lowered her voice. "But I know my duty. He says that in the next world we'll be together." She didn't want to tell the rest of it, the remarkable things she'd seen with the stranger, the way she'd *recognized* him. The way they were destined for each other.

"And you believed him? Oh, my dear child. You're so innocent. I suppose that comes from living your life in a temple." She gazed around thoughtfully, then looked back at Hannah. Her face became grave and regretful.

"I hate to have to tell you this," she said. "But the stranger does *not* love you. The truth is that he's a very evil man. The truth is that he's not a man at all. He's an Ur-Demon and he wants to steal your *sa.*"

Oh, Isis, Ha-nahkt thought. *Sa* was the breath of life, the magical force that allowed you to live. She'd heard of demons who wanted to steal it. But she couldn't believe it of the stranger. He seemed so gentle, so kind . . .

"It's true," Maya said positively. She glanced at Ha-nahkt sideways. "And you know it is, if you think about it. Why else would he want to taste your blood?"

Ha-nahkt started and flushed. "How do you know—?" She stopped and bit her lip.

"You've been meeting him at night by the lotus pool, when everyone else is asleep," Maya said. "And I suppose you thought it wouldn't hurt to let him drink a little of your blood. Not much. Just a bit. It was exciting. But I'm telling you the truth, now—it *will* hurt you. He's a demon and he wants you dead."

The husky, mesmerizing voice went on and on. It was telling all about Ur-Demons who drank blood, and men and women who could change into animals, and a place called the World of the Night, where they all lived. Ha-nahkt's head began to spin.

And her heart shattered.

Literally. She could feel the jagged pieces of it every time she tried to breathe. A priestess didn't cry, but tears were forcing themselves out of her closed lids.

Because she couldn't deny that the stranger did act a little like an Ur-Demon. Why else *would* he drink blood?

And the things she'd seen with him, the feeling of destiny . . . that must have all been magic. He had tricked her with spells.

Maya seemed to have finished her story. "Do you think you can remember all that?" she asked.

Ha-nahkt made a miserable gesture. What did it matter if she remembered it? She only wanted to be left alone.

"Look at me!"

Ha-nahkt glanced up, startled. It was a mistake. Maya's eyes were strange; they seemed to turn different colors from moment to moment, and once Ha-nahkt met them, she couldn't look away. She was caught in a spell, and she felt her will slipping.

"Now," Maya said, and her eyes were deep gold and ancient as a crocodile's. "Remember all that. And remember this. Remember . . . how he kills you."

And then the strangest thing of all happened.

It suddenly seemed to Ha-nahkt that she was two people. One of them was her ordinary self. And the other was a different self, a distant self, who seemed to be looking on from the future. At this moment, Ha-nahkt and the future self were seeing different things.

Ha-nahkt saw that Maya was gone and the temple was empty. And then she saw that someone else was walking in. A tall figure, with light hair and dark fathomless eyes—the stranger. He smiled at her, walked toward her with his arms held out. He grasped her with hands that were as strong as a demon's. Then he showed his teeth.

The future self saw something else. She saw that Maya never left the temple. She saw Maya's face and body ripple as if they were made of water—and then change. It was as if there were two images, one on top of the other. The outward image was of the stranger, but it was Maya underneath.

That's it. That's how she did it.

The voice came from outside Ha-nahkt, and she didn't understand it. She didn't have time to think about it, either, because the next instant she felt the tearing pain of teeth.

Oh, Isis, Goddess of Life, guide me to the other world. . . .

"That's how she did it," Hannah breathed.

She was sitting up on the couch. She knew who she was, and more, she knew who she'd been.

It was another of those blinding flashes of illumination. She felt as if she were standing at the end of the corridor of time and looking back at a hundred different versions of herself. They each looked slightly different, and they wore different clothes, but they were all her. Her name had been Hanje, Anora, Xiana, Nan Haiane, Honni, Ian, Annette. She had been a warrior, a priestess, a princess, a slave. And right now she felt she had the strength of all her selves.

At the far end of the corridor, back where it was misty and blurry and faintly tinted pink and blue, she seemed to see Hana smiling at her. And then Hana turned and walked away, her task accomplished.

Hannah took a deep breath and let it out.

"She did it with illusions," she said, hardly aware that she was talking out loud. "Maya. And she's done it before, of course. Maybe every time. What do you do with somebody who keeps killing you over and over? Never letting you live to your seventeenth birthday? Trying to destroy you, not just your life, but your heart . . . ?"

She realized that Paul was staring at her. "You want me to answer that?"

Hannah shook her head even as she went on talking. "Goddess—I mean, God—she must hate me. I still don't understand why. It must be because she wants Thierry herself—or maybe just because she wants him miserable. She wants him to know that I'm terrified of him, that I hate him. And she *did* it. She convinced me. She convinced my subconscious enough that I started warning myself against him."

"If any of this is true—which I'm not going to admit for a second, because they would definitely take my license away—then I can tell you one thing," Paul said. "She sounds very, very dangerous."

"She is."

"Then why are you so happy?" he asked pathetically.

Hannah glanced at him and laughed. She couldn't hope to explain it.

But she was more than happy, she was exalted. She was buoyant, ecstatic, over the moon.

Thierry wasn't evil. She had the confirmation of a hundred selves whispering it to her. Maya was the enemy, the snake in the garden. Thierry was exactly what he'd told her he was. Someone who had made a terrible mistake and had spent millennia paying for it—and searching for her.

He *is* gentle and kind. He does love me. And we *are* destined for each other.

I've got to find him.

The last thought came as an additional bright revelation, but one that made her sit up and go still.

She had no idea how.

Where had he gone? Home. Where was home? She didn't know.

It could be anywhere in the world.

"Hannah . . ."

"Wait," Hannah whispered.

"Look, Hannah, I think we should maybe do some work on this. Talk about it, examine your feelings . . ."

"No, hush!" Hannah waved a hand at him. "She gave me a clue! She didn't mean to, but she gave me a clue! She said he had connections with witches in Vegas."

"Oh, my God," Paul muttered. Then he jumped up. "Hannah, where are you going?"

"I'm sorry." She darted back into the office, threw her arms around him, and gave him a kiss. Then, smiling into his startled face, she said, "Thank you. Thank you for helping. You'll never know how much you've done for me."

"I need money."

Chess blinked, but went on looking at her intently.

"I know it isn't fair to ask you without explaining why. But I *can't* tell you. It would be dangerous for you. I just have to ask you to trust me."

Chess kept looking at her. The slanted green eyes searched Hannah's face. Then, without a word, she got up.

Hannah sat on Chess's crisp white-on-white coverlet and waited. After a few minutes Chess came back into the room and settled her own petite self on the bed.

"Here," she said, and plunked down a credit card. "Mom

said I could use it to get some things for graduation. I figure she'll understand—maybe."

Hannah threw her arms around her. "Thank you," she whispered. "I'll pay it back as soon as I can." Then she burst out, "How can you be so nice? I'd be yelling to know what was going on."

"I *am* going to yell," Chess said, squeezing her back. "But more than that. I'm going with you."

Hannah drew back. How could she explain? She knew that by going to Las Vegas she would be putting her own life in danger. From Maya, certainly. From the Night World, probably. Even from the witches Thierry had connections with, possibly.

And she couldn't drag Chess into that.

"I've got something I want you to hang on to," she said. She reached into her canvas bag and pulled out an envelope. "This is for you and for my mom—just in case. If you don't hear from me by my birthday, then I want you to open it."

"Didn't you hear me? I'm going *with* you. I don't know what's been going on with you, but I'm not going to let you run off on your own."

"And I can't take you." She caught the glowing cat-eyes and held them. "Please understand, Chess. It's something I have to do alone. Besides, I need you here to cover for me, to tell my mom I'm at your house so she doesn't worry. Okay?" She reached out and gave Chess a tiny shake. "Okay?"

Chess shut her eyes, then nodded. Then she sniffled, her chin trembling.

Hannah hugged her again. "Thank you," she whispered. "Let's be best friends forever."

Monday morning, instead of going to school, Hannah started for Billings airport. She was driving the Ford—her mom had fixed it over the weekend. Her mom thought she was spending the next couple of days with Chess to study for finals.

It was frightening but exhilarating to fly on a plane by herself, going to a city she'd never been to before. All the time she was in the air, she was thinking, Closer, closer, closer—and looking at the black rose ring on her finger.

She'd fished it out of her bedroom wastebasket. Now she turned her hand this way and that to see the black gems catch the light. Her chest tightened.

What if I can't find him? she thought.

The other fear she didn't want to admit, even to herself. What if she did find him, and he didn't want her anymore? After all, she'd only told him that she hated him a few dozen times and ordered him to stay away from her forever.

I won't think about that. There's no point. First I have to track him down, and after that what happens, happens.

The airport in Las Vegas was surprisingly small. There were slot machines all over. Hannah collected her one duffel bag at the luggage carousel and then walked outside. She stood in the warm desert air, trying to figure out what to do next.

How do you find witches?

She didn't know. She didn't think they were likely to be listed in the phone book. So she just trusted to luck and headed where everybody else was heading—the Strip.

It was a mistake from the beginning, and that afternoon and night were among the worst times in her life.

It didn't start off so bad. The Strip was gaudy and glittery, especially as darkness fell. The hotels were so bizarre and so dazzling that it took Hannah's breath away. One of them, the Luxor, was shaped like a giant black pyramid with a Sphinx in front of it. Hannah stood and watched colored lasers dart from the Sphinx's eyes and laughed.

What would Ha-nahkt have thought of *that*?

But there was something almost sickening about all the lights and the hustling after a while. Something . . . unwholesome. The crowds were so thick, both inside the hotels and out on the street, that Hannah could hardly move. Everyone seemed to be in a rush—except the people nailed in front of slot machines.

It feels . . . greedy, Hannah decided finally, searching in her mind for the right word. All these people want to win free money. All these hotels want to take their money. And of course, the hotels are the winners in the end. They've built a sort of Venus flytrap to lure people here. And some of these people don't look as if they can afford to lose.

Her heart felt physically heavy and her lungs felt constricted. She wanted Montana and a horizon so far away that it pried your mind open. She wanted clean air. She wanted *space*.

But even worse than the atmosphere of greed and commercialism was the fact that she wasn't finding any witches.

She struck up conversations a few times with desk clerks and waitresses. But when she casually asked if there were any odd people in town who practiced witchcraft, they looked at her as if she were crazy.

By nine o'clock that night she was dizzy, exhausted, and sick with defeat.

I'm never going to find them. Which means I'm never going to find him.

She collapsed on a bench outside the Stardust Hotel, wondering what to do next. Her legs hurt and her head was pounding. She didn't want to spend Chess's mom's money on a hotel—but she'd noticed police officers making people move on if they tried to sleep on the street.

Why did I come here? I should have put an ad in the paper: "Desperately Seeking Thierry." I should have known this wouldn't work.

Even as she was thinking it, something about a boy in the crowd caught her eye.

He wasn't Thierry. He wasn't anything like Thierry. Except for the way he moved.

It was that same rippling grace she'd seen in both Thierry

and Maya, an easy control of motion that reminded her of a jungle cat. And his face . . . he was almost eerily good-looking in a ragamuffin way.

When he glanced up toward the Stardust's tall neon sign, she thought she could see light reflect from his eyes.

He's one of them. I know it. He's one of the Night People.

Without stopping to think, she jumped up, slung her bag over her shoulder, and followed him.

It wasn't easy. He walked fast and she had to keep dodging tourists. He was headed off the Strip, to one of the quiet dimly-lit streets that ran parallel to it.

It was a whole different world here, just one block away from the glitter and bustle. The hotels were small and in poor repair. The businesses seemed to be mostly pawnshops. Everything had a dingy, depressed feeling.

Hannah felt a prickling down her spine.

She was now following the only figure on a deserted street. Any minute now, he'd realize she was tailing him—but what could she do? She didn't dare lose sight of him.

The boy seemed to be leading her into worse and worse areas—*sleazy* was the word for them, Hannah thought. The streetlights were far apart here with areas of darkness in between.

All at once he took a sharp left turn, seeming to disappear behind a building with a sign that read, DAN'S BAIL BONDS. Hannah jogged to catch up to him and found herself staring down a narrow alley. It was extremely dark. She hesitated a moment, then grimly took a few steps forward.

On the third step, the boy appeared from behind a Dumpster.

He was facing her, and once again Hannah caught the flash of eyeshine. She stood very still as he walked slowly toward her.

"You following me or something?" he asked. He seemed amused. He had a sharp face with an almost pointed chin and dark hair that looked uncombed. He was no taller than Hannah, but his body seemed tough and wiry.

It's the Artful Dodger, Hannah thought.

As he reached her, he looked her up and down. His expression was a combination of lechery and hunger. Gooseflesh blossomed on Hannah's skin.

"I'm sorry," she said, trying to make her voice quiet and direct. "I *was* following you. I wanted to ask you something— I'm looking for someone."

"You found him, baby," the boy said. He darted a quick glance around as if to make sure that there was nobody in the alley with them.

And then, before Hannah could say another word, he knocked her into the wall and pinned her there.

CHAPTER 13

"Don't fight," he panted into her face. "It'll be easier if you just relax."

Hannah was frightened—and furious. "In your dreams," she gasped and slammed a knee into his groin. She hadn't survived Maya and come thousands of miles to be killed by some weasel of a vampire.

She could feel him trying to do something to her mind—it reminded her of the way Maya had captured Ha-nahkt's eyes. Some kind of hypnosis, she supposed. But she'd had enough of hypnosis in the last week. She fought it.

And she fought with her body, unskillfully maybe, but with utter conviction. She head-butted him on the nose when he tried to get close to her neck.

"Ow!" The Artful Dodger jerked back. Then he got a better grip on her arm. He pulled the wrist toward him and Hannah suddenly realized what he was doing. There were nice, accessible veins there. He was going to draw blood from her wrist.

"No, you don't," she gasped. She had no idea what would happen if she lost any more blood to a vampire. Thierry had said she wasn't in danger as long as she kept away from them for the next week, so she presumed that if she didn't stay away, she *was* in danger. And she was already noticing little changes in herself: her ability to see better in the dark, for instance.

She tried to wrench her arm out of the boy's grip—and then she heard a gasp. Suddenly she realized that he wasn't holding her as tightly, and he wasn't trying to pull her wrist to him. Instead he was just staring at her hand.

At her ring.

The expression on his face might have been funny if Hannah hadn't been shaking with adrenaline. He looked shocked, dismayed, scared, disbelieving, and embarrassed all at once.

"Who—who—who *are* you?" he spluttered.

Hannah looked at the ring, and then at him. Of course. How could she have been so stupid? She should have mentioned Thierry right away. If he was a Lord of the Night World, maybe everybody knew him. Maybe she could skip the witches altogether.

"I told you I was looking for somebody. His name is Thierry Descouedres. He gave me this ring."

The Artful Dodger gave a kind of moan. Then he looked

up at her from under his spiky bangs. "I didn't hurt you, did
I?" he said. It wasn't a question, it was a demand for agreement.
"I didn't do anything to you."

"You didn't get the chance," Hannah said. But she was
afraid the boy might just take off running, so she added, "I
don't want to get you in trouble. I just want to find Thierry.
Can you help me?"

"I . . . help you. Yeah, yeah. I can be a big help." He hesitated, then said, "It's kind of a long walk."

A walk? Thierry was *here*? Hannah's heart leaped so high
that her whole body felt light.

"I'm not tired," she said, and it was true. "I can walk anywhere."

The house was enormous.

Magnificent. Palatial, even. Awe-inspiring.

The Artful Dodger abandoned Hannah at the beginning
of the long palm-tree-lined drive, blurting, "That's it," and
then scampering off into the darkness. Hannah looked after
him for a moment, then grimly started up the drive, sincerely
hoping that it *was* it. She was so tired that she was weaving and
her feet felt as if they'd been pounded with stones.

As she walked up to the front door, though, her doubts
disappeared. There were black roses everywhere.

There was an arch-shaped stained-glass window above the
double doors, showing a black rose that had the same intri-

cately knotted stem as the one on Hannah's ring. The same design had been worked into the crowns over the windows. It was used like a family crest or seal.

Just seeing all those roses made Hannah's heart beat faster.

Okay, then. Ring the doorbell, she told herself. And stop feeling like some Cinderella who's come to see what's keeping the prince.

She pushed the doorbell button, then held her breath as chimes echoed distantly.

Please. Please answer. . . .

She heard footsteps approaching and her heart *really* started to pound.

I can't believe it's all been this easy. . . .

But when the door opened, it wasn't Thierry. It was a college-age guy with a suit, brown hair pulled back into a short ponytail, and dark glasses. He looked vaguely like a young CIA agent, Hannah thought wildly.

He and Hannah stared at each other.

"Uh, I'm here to . . . I'm looking for Thierry Descouedres," Hannah said finally, trying to sound confident.

The CIA guy didn't change expression. When he spoke, it wasn't unkindly, but Hannah's heart plummeted.

"He's not here. Try again in a few days. And it's better to call one of his secretaries before showing up."

He started to shut the door.

A wave of desperation broke over Hannah.

"Wait!" she said, and she actually stuck her foot in the doorway. She was amazed at herself.

The CIA guy looked down at her foot, then up at her face. "Yes?"

Oh, God, he thinks I'm a nuisance visitor. Hannah suddenly had a vision of swarms of petitioners lined up at Thierry's house, all wanting him to do something for them. Like supplicants waiting for an audience with the king.

And I must look like riffraff, she thought. She was wearing Levis and a shirt that was sweaty and wrinkled after tramping around the Strip all day. Her boots were dusty. Her hair was limp and disheveled, straggling over her face.

"Yes?" the CIA guy said again, politely urgent.

"I . . . nothing." Hannah felt tears spring to her eyes and was furious with herself. She hid them by bending down to pick up her duffel bag, which by now felt as if it were loaded with rocks.

She had never been so tired. Her mouth was dry and cottony and her muscles were starting to cramp. She had no idea where to find a safe place to sleep.

But it wasn't the CIA guy's problem.

"Thank you," Hannah said. She took a deep breath and started to turn away.

It was the deep breath that did it. Someone was crossing the grand entrance hall behind the CIA guy and the breath delayed Hannah long enough that they saw each other.

"Nilsson, *wait!*" the someone yelled and came bounding over to the door.

It was a girl, thin and tanned, with odd silvery-brown hair and dark amber eyes. She had several yellowing bruises on her face.

But it was her expression that startled Hannah. Her amber eyes were wide and sparkling in what looked like recognition, her mouth was open in astonishment and excitement. She was waving her arms.

"That's her!" she yelled at the CIA guy, pointing to Hannah. "It's her! It's *her*." When he stared at her, she hit him in the shoulder. *"Her!"*

They both turned to stare at Hannah. The CIA guy had an expression now. He looked stunned.

Hannah stared back at them, bewildered.

Then, seeming dazed, the CIA guy very slowly opened the door. "My name is Nilsson, miss," he said. "Please come inside."

Stupid me, Hannah thought. Almost as an afterthought, she pushed straggling hair off her left cheek, away from her birthmark. I should have told them who I was. But how could I know they would understand?

Nilsson was talking again as he gently took her bag. "I'm very sorry, miss—I didn't realize . . . I hope you won't hold this—"

"Nobody knew you were *coming*," the girl broke in with

refreshing bluntness. "And the worst thing is that Thierry's gone off somewhere. I don't think anybody knows where or when he'll be back. But meanwhile you'd better stay put. I don't want to think about what he'd do to us if we lost you." She smiled at Hannah and added, "I'm Lupe Acevedo."

"Hannah Snow."

"I know." The girl winked. "We met before, but I couldn't exactly introduce myself. Don't you remember?"

Hannah started to shake her head—and then she blinked. Blinked again. That silvery-brown coloring . . . those amber eyes . . .

"Yeah," Lupe said, looking hugely delighted. "That was me. That's how I got these bruises. The other wolf got it worse, though. I ripped him a new—"

"Would you like something to drink?" Nilsson interrupted hastily. "Or to eat? Why don't you come in and sit down?"

Hannah's mind was reeling. That girl is a werewolf, she thought. A *werewolf.* The last time I saw her she had big ears and a bushy tail. Werewolves are real.

And this one protected me.

She said dizzily, "I . . . thank you. I mean, you saved my life, didn't you?"

Lupe shrugged. "Part of the job. Want a Coke?"

Hannah blinked, then laughed. "I'd kill for one."

"I'll take care of it," Nilsson said. "I'll take care of everything. Lupe, why don't you show her upstairs?" He hurried off and opened a cellular phone. A moment later several other guys dressed like him came running. The strange thing was that they were all very young—all in their late teens. Hannah caught snatches of frantic-sounding conversation.

"Well, try *that* number—"

"What about leaving a message with—"

"Come on," Lupe said, interrupting Hannah's eavesdropping. With that same cheerful bluntness she added, "You look like you could use a bath."

She led Hannah past a giant white sculpture toward a wide curving staircase. Hannah glimpsed other rooms opening off the hallway. A living room that looked as big as a football field, decorated with white couches, geometric furniture, and abstract paintings. A dining room with a mile-long table. An alcove with a grand piano.

Hannah felt more like Cinderella than ever. Nobody in Medicine Rock had a grand piano.

I didn't know he was so rich. I don't know if I can deal with this.

But when she was installed in a sort of Moorish fantasy bathroom, surrounded by jungly green plants and exotic tiles and brass globe lights with cut-out star shapes, she decided that she could probably adjust to living this way. If forced.

It was heaven just to relax in the Jacuzzi tub, drinking a Coke and breathing in the delicious scent of bath salts. And it was even better to sit up in bed afterward, eating finger sandwiches sent up by "Chef" and telling Lupe how she came to be in Las Vegas.

When she was done, Lupe said, "Nilsson and everybody are trying to find Thierry. It may take a little while, though. See, he just stopped off for a few minutes on Saturday, and then he disappeared again. But meanwhile, this house is pretty well protected. And all of us will fight for you—I mean, fight to the death, if we have to. So it's safer than most other places."

Hannah felt a roiling in her stomach. She didn't understand. Lupe made it sound as if they were in some castle getting ready for a siege. "Safe from . . . ?"

Lupe looked surprised. "From *her*—Maya," she said, as if it should be obvious.

Hannah had a sinking feeling. I should have known, she thought. But all she said was, "So you think I'm still in danger from her."

Lupe's eyebrows shot up. She said mildly, "Well, sure. She's going to try to kill you. And she's awfully good at killing."

Especially me, Hannah thought. But she was too tired to be much afraid. Trusting to Lupe and Nilsson and the rest of Thierry's household, she fell asleep that night as soon as her head touched the pillow.

She woke up to see sunshine. It was reflecting off the bedroom walls, which were painted a softly burnished gold. Weird but beautiful, Hannah thought, looking dreamily around at ebony furniture and decorative tribal masks. Then she remembered where she was and jumped out of bed.

She found clean clothes—her size—lying on an elaborately carved chest. She had just finished pulling them on when Lupe knocked on the door.

"Lupe, have they—"

Lupe shook her silvery-brown head. "They haven't found him yet."

Hannah sighed, then smiled, trying not to look too disappointed.

Lupe made a sympathetic face. "I know. While you wait, though, you might like to meet some people." She grinned. "They're sort of special people, and it's a secret that they're even here. But I talked to them last night, and they all decided that it would be okay. They all want to meet you."

Hannah was curious. "Special people? Are they humans or . . . uh . . . ?"

Lupe grinned even more widely. "They're both. That's why they're special." As she talked, she was leading Hannah downstairs and through miles of hallway. "They did something for me," she said, not smiling now, but serious. "They saved my life and my mom's life. See, I'm not a purebred werewolf. My dad was human."

Hannah looked at her, startled.

"Yeah. And that's against the laws of the Night World. You can't fall in love with a human, much less marry them.

The other werewolves came one night and killed my dad. They would have killed my mom and me, too, but Thierry got us out of the city and hid us. That's why I'd do anything for him. I wouldn't be alive if it wasn't for him . . . and Circle Daybreak."

She had paused by the door of a room located toward the back of the house. Now, she opened the door, gave Hannah a funny little nod and a wink, and said, "You go meet them. I think you'll like each other. You're their type."

Hannah wasn't sure what this meant. She felt shy as she stepped over the threshold and looked around the room.

It was a den, smaller than the front living room, and more cozy, with furniture in warm ochers and burnt siennas. A breakfast buffet was set out on a long sideboard made of golden pine. It smelled good, but Hannah didn't have time to look at it. As soon as she came in the room, every head turned and she found a dozen people staring at her.

Young people. All around her age. Normal-type teenagers, except that a surprising number of them were extremely good-looking.

Behind her, the door closed firmly. Hannah felt more and more as if she'd just walked out onstage and forgotten her lines.

Then one of the girls sitting on an ottoman jumped up and ran to her. "You're Hana, aren't you?" she said warmly.

"Hannah. Yes."

"I can't believe I'm really meeting you! This is so exciting. Thierry's told us all about you." She put a gentle hand on Hannah's arm. "Hannah, this is Circle Daybreak. And my name is Thea Harman."

She was almost as tall as Hannah was, and the yellow hair spilling over her shoulders was a few shades darker than Hannah's. Her eyes were brown and soft and somehow wise.

"Hi, Thea." Somehow Hannah felt instinctively at ease with this girl. "Lupe was telling me about Circle Daybreak, but I didn't exactly understand."

"It started as a sort of witch organization," Thea said. "A witch circle. But it's not just for witches. It's for humans and vampires and werewolves and shapeshifters . . . and, well, anybody who wants to help Night People and humans get along. Come and meet the others and we'll try to explain."

A few minutes later, Hannah was sitting on a couch with a plate of eggs Benedict, being introduced.

"This is James and Poppy," Thea said. "James is a Redfern on his mother's side—which makes him a descendant of Maya's." She glanced at James with gentle mischief.

"I didn't pick my parents. Believe me, I didn't," James said to Hannah. He had light brown hair and thoughtful gray eyes. When he smiled it was impossible not to smile back.

"Nobody would have picked your parents, Jamie," Poppy said, elbowing him. She was very small, but there was a kind of impish wisdom in her face. Her head was a tangle of copper curls and her eyes were as green as emeralds. Hannah found her elfin beauty just a little scary . . . just a little inhuman.

"They're both vampires," Thea said, answering Hannah's unspoken question.

"I didn't used to be," Poppy said. "James changed me because I was dying."

"What's a soulmate for?" James said, and Poppy poked him again and then grinned at him. They were obviously in love.

"You're—soulmates?" Hannah spoke softly, wistfully.

It was Thea who answered. "That's the thing, you see— something is causing Night People to find human soul- mates. We witches think that it's some Power that's waking up again, making it happen. Some Power that's been asleep for a long time—maybe since the time when Thierry was born."

Now Hannah understood why Lupe had said she was Circle Daybreak's type of people. She was part of this.

"But—that's wonderful," she said, speaking slowly and try- ing to gather her thoughts. "I mean . . ." She couldn't exactly explain *why* it was so wonderful, but she had a sense of some immense turning point being reached in the world, of some cycle that was about to end.

Thea was smiling at her. "I know what you mean. We think so, too." She turned and held out a hand to a very tall boy with a sweet face, sandy hair, and hazel eyes. "And this is *my* soulmate, Eric. He's human."

"Just barely," a boy from the other side of the room said. Eric ignored him and smiled at Hannah.

"And this is Gillian and David," Thea said, moving around the circle. "Gillian's a distant cousin of mine, a witch, and David's human. Soulmates, again."

Gillian was tiny, with white-blond hair that fit her head like a silky cap and deep violet eyes. David had dark hair, brown eyes, and a lean tanned face. They both smiled at Hannah.

Thea was moving on. "And next comes Rashel and Quinn. Rashel is human—she used to be a vampire hunter."

"I still am. But now I just hunt *bad* vampires," Rashel said coolly. Hannah had an instinctive feeling of respect for her. She was tall and seemed to have perfect control of her body. Her hair was black and her eyes were a fierce and blazing green.

"And Quinn's a vampire," Thea said.

Quinn was the boy who'd made the barely-human remark. He was very good-looking, with clean features that were strongly chiseled but almost delicate. His hair was as black as Rashel's, and his eyes were black, too. He flashed Hannah a smile that, while beautiful, was slightly unnerving.

"Quinn's the only one here who can compete with you as far as the past goes," Thea added. "He was made into a vampire back in the sixteen hundreds, by Hunter Redfern."

Quinn flashed another smile. "Did you have a life in colonial America? Maybe we've met."

Hannah smiled in return, but she was also studying him with interest. He didn't look older than eighteen.

"Is that why everybody here looks so young?" she asked. "All the staff, I mean—Nilsson and the other guys in suits. Are they all vampires?"

Thea nodded. "All made vampires. Lamia, like James, can grow up if they want. But once you make a human into a vampire they stop aging—and you can't make somebody over nineteen into a vampire. Their bodies can't make the change. They just burn out."

Hannah felt an odd chill, almost of premonition. But before she could say anything, a new voice interrupted.

"Speaking of the lamia, isn't anybody going to introduce *me*?"

Thea turned toward the window. "Sorry, Ash—but if you're going to sleep over there, you can't blame us for forgetting you." She looked at Hannah. "This is another Redfern, a cousin of James's. His name is Ash."

Ash was gorgeous, lanky and elegant, with ash-blond hair. But what startled Hannah as he got up and unhurriedly walked to meet her was his eyes.

They were like Maya's eyes, shifting color from moment to moment. The resemblance was so striking that it was a moment before Hannah could take his hand.

He's got Maya's genes, Hannah thought. He smiled at her, then sprawled on the love seat.

"We're not all of Circle Daybreak, of course," Thea said. "In fact, we're some of the newest members. And we're from all over the country—North Carolina, Pennsylvania, Massachusetts, everywhere. But Thierry called us together specially, to talk about the soulmate principle and the old Powers awakening."

"That was last week, before he found out about you," copper-haired Poppy said. "And before he ran off. But we've been talking without him, trying to figure out what to do next."

Hannah said, "Whatever it is, I'd like to help you."

They all looked pleased. But Thea said, "You should think about it first. We're dangerous people to know."

"We're on everybody's hit list," Rashel, the black-haired vampire hunter, said dryly.

"We've got the whole Night World against us," Ash said, rolling his ever-changing eyes.

"Against *us*. You just said 'us.'" James turned on his cousin triumphantly, as if he'd just won a point in an argument. "You admit you're a part of us."

Ash looked at the ceiling. "I don't have any choice."

"But *you* do, Hannah," Thea interrupted. She smiled at Hannah, but her soft brown eyes were serious. "You don't have to be in any more danger than you are now."

"I think—" Hannah began. But before she could finish, there was an explosion of noise from somewhere outside.

CHAPTER 14

Stay here," Rashel said sharply, but Hannah ran with the rest of them toward the front of the house. She could hear a ferocious snarling and barking outside—a very familiar sort of sound.

Nilsson and the other CIA guys were running around. They looked grim and efficient, moving fast but not frantically. Hannah realized that they knew how to do this sort of thing.

She didn't see Lupe.

The snarling outside got louder, building to a volley of short barks. There was a yelp—and then a scrambling noise. After a moment of silence there came a sound that lifted the hair on Hannah's forearms—a wild and eerie and beautiful sound. A wolf howling. Two other wolf voices joined the first, chording, rising and falling, interweaving with each other. Hannah found herself gasping, her entire skin shivering. Then there was one long sustained note and it was over.

"Wow," the tiny blond called Gillian whispered.

Hannah rubbed her bare arms hard.

The front door opened. Hannah felt herself looking toward the ground, but nothing four-legged came in. Instead it was Lupe and two guys, all disheveled, flushed, and grinning.

"It was just some scouts," Lupe said. "We ran them off."

"Scouts from Maya?" Hannah said, feeling a tightness in her stomach. It really was true, then. Maya was trying to storm the house to get to her.

Lupe nodded. "It'll be okay," she said almost gently. "But I think all of you better stay inside today. You can watch movies or play games in the game room."

Hannah spent the day talking with the Circle Daybreak members. The more she found out about them, the more she liked them. Only one thing made her uncomfortable. They all seemed to defer to her—as if, somehow, they expected her to be wiser or better because of her former lifetimes. It was embarrassing, because she knew she wasn't.

She tried to keep her mind off Thierry . . . and Maya.

But it wasn't easy. That night she found herself walking restlessly through the house. She wound up in a little anteroom on the second floor that looked down on the enormous living room.

"Can't relax?"

The lazy murmur came from behind her. Hannah turned to see Ash, his lanky elegant body propped against a wall. His eyes looked silver in the dimly lit room.

"Not really," Hannah admitted. "I just wish they'd find Thierry. I've got a bad feeling about it."

They stood for a moment in silence. Then Ash said, "Yeah, it's hard to be without your soulmate. Once you've found them, I mean."

Hannah looked at him, intrigued. The way he said that . . .

She spoke hesitantly. "This morning Thea said you were all here because you had human soulmates."

He looked across the room at French doors that led to a balcony. "Yes?"

"And—well . . ." Maybe she's *dead*, Hannah thought suddenly. Maybe I shouldn't ask.

"And you want to know where mine is," Ash said.

"I didn't mean to pry."

"No. It's okay." Ash looked out at the darkness beyond the French doors again. "She's waiting—I hope. I've got some things to put right before I see her."

He didn't seem scary anymore, no matter how his eyes changed. He seemed—vulnerable.

"I'm sure she *is* waiting," Hannah said. "And I'll bet she'll be glad to see you when you've put things right." She added quietly, "I know I'll be glad to see Thierry."

He glanced at her, startled, then smiled. He had a very nice smile. "That's true, you've been in her shoes, haven't you? And Thierry's certainly tried to make up for his past. I mean, he's been doing good works for centuries. So maybe there's hope for me after all."

He said it almost mockingly, but Hannah caught an odd glistening in his eyes.

"You're like her, you know," he added abruptly. "Like my—like Mary-Lynnette. You're both . . . wise."

Before Hannah could think of something to say to that, he nodded to her, straightened up, and went back into the hallway, whistling softly through his teeth.

Hannah stood alone in the dim room. For some reason, she felt better suddenly. More optimistic about the future.

I think I'll be able to sleep tonight. And tomorrow, maybe Thierry will be here.

She clamped down hard on the rush of hope that filled her at the thought. Hope . . . and concern. After all she'd said to him, she couldn't be absolutely sure how Thierry would receive her.

What if he doesn't want me after all?

Don't be silly. Don't *think* about it. Go outside and get a breath of air, and then go to bed.

Later, of course, she realized just how stupid she had been. She should have known that getting a breath of fresh air only led to one thing in her life.

But at the moment it seemed like a good idea. Lupe had warned her not to open any outside doors—but the French doors only led to a second-floor balcony overlooking the backyard. Hannah opened them and stepped out.

Nice, she thought. The air was just cool enough to be pleasant.

From here she could look across dark stretches of grass to flood-lit palm trees and softly splashing fountains. Although she couldn't see Thierry's people, she knew they were out there, stationed around the grounds, watching and waiting. Guarding her. It made her feel safe.

Nothing can get to the house with them around it, she thought. I can sleep just fine.

She was about to turn and go back inside when she heard the scratching.

It came from above her. From the roof. She glanced up and got the shock of this particular lifetime.

There was a bat hanging from the roof.

A bat. A *bat*.

A huge bat. Upside down. Its leathery black wings were wrapped around it and its small red eyes shone at her with reflected light.

Wild thoughts tumbled through Hannah's mind, all in a fraction of an instant. Maybe it's a decoration . . . no, idiot, it's *alive*. Maybe it's somebody to guard me. God, maybe it's *Thierry*. . . .

But all the while, she knew. And when the instant of paralysis passed and she could command her body again, she sucked in a deep breath to scream an alarm.

She never got the chance to make a sound. With a noise

like an umbrella opening, the bat unfolded its wings suddenly, displaying an amazingly large span of black membrane.

At the same moment something like sheet lightning seemed to hit Hannah, a blinding surge of pure mental energy. She saw stars, and then everything faded to darkness.

Something hurt.

My head, Hannah thought slowly. And my back.

In fact, she hurt all over. And she was blind—or she had her eyes shut. She tried to open them and nothing changed. She could feel herself blinking, but she could only see one thing.

Blackness. Utter, complete blackness.

She realized then that she'd never seen real darkness before. In her bedroom at night there was always some diffused light showing at the top of her curtains. Even outdoors there was always moonlight or starlight, or if it were cloudy, the reflection of human lights, however faint.

This was different. This was *solid* darkness. Hannah imagined she could feel it pressing against her face, weighing down on her body. And no matter how wide she opened her eyes or how fixedly she stared, she couldn't see even the slightest glimmer breaking it

I will not panic, she told herself.

But it was hard. She was fighting an instinctive fear, hardwired into the brain since before the Stone Age. All humans panicked in complete blackness.

Just breathe, she told herself firmly. *Breathe.* Okay. Now. You've got to get out of here. First things first. Are you hurt?

She couldn't tell. She had to shut her eyes in order to sense her own body. As she did, she realized that she was sitting up, instinctively huddling into herself to keep safe from the darkness.

Okay. I don't think you're hurt. Let's try standing up. Very slowly.

That was when the real shock came.

She couldn't stand up.

She *couldn't.*

She could move her arms and even her legs. But when she tried to lift her body, even to shift position slightly, something bit into her waist, keeping her immobile.

With a crawling feeling of horror, Hannah put her hands to her waist and felt the rough texture of rope.

I'm tied. I'm *tied. . . .*

There was something hard against her back. A tree? Her hands flew to feel it. No, not a tree—too regular. Tall, but squarish. A post of some kind.

The rope seemed to be wound many times around her waist, tightly enough that it constricted her breathing a little. It bound her securely to the post. And then it fastened above or far behind her somewhere—she couldn't find any knots with her fingers.

It felt like very strong, very sturdy rope. Hannah knew

without question that she wasn't going to be able to wiggle out of it or untie it.

The post seemed very sturdy, too. The ground under Hannah was dirt and rock.

I'm alone, she thought slowly. She could hear her own gasping breath. I'm all alone . . . and I'm tied here in the dark. I can't move. *I can't get away.*

Maya put me here. She left me to die all alone in the dark.

For a while, then, Hannah simply lost control. She screamed for help and heard her voice echo oddly. She pulled and twisted at the rope with her fingers until her fingertips were raw. She threw her whole body from one side to the other, trying to loosen the rope or the post, until the pain in her waist made her stop. And finally she gave in to the galloping fear inside her and sobbed out loud.

She had never, ever, felt so desolate and alone.

In the end, though, she cried herself out. And when she'd gasped to a stop, she found that she could think a little.

Listen, girl. You've got to get a grip. You've got to help yourself, because there's nobody else to do it.

It wasn't the cool wind voice or even the crystal voice—because they were both just part of her now. It was Hannah's own mental voice. She had accepted all her past selves and their experiences, and in return she felt she could call on at least some of their wisdom.

Okay, she thought grimly. No more crying. Think. What can you tell about your situation?

I'm not out in the open. I know because there's no light at all and because of the way my voice echoed. I'm in a big . . . room or something. It's got a high ceiling. And the floor is rock.

Good. Okay, do you hear anything else?

Hannah listened. It was hard to concentrate on the silence around her—it made her own breathing and heartbeat seem terrifyingly loud. She could feel her nerves stretch and fray . . . but she held on, ignoring her own noises and trying to reach out into the darkness with her ears.

Then she heard it. Very far away, a sound like a faucet dripping slowly.

What the hell? I'm in a big black room with a rock floor and a leaky faucet.

Shut up. Keep concentrating. What do you smell?

Hannah sniffed. That didn't work, so she took long breaths through her nose, ignoring the pain as her midsection pressed against the rope.

It's musty in here. Dank. It smells damp and cold.

In fact, it was very cold. Her panic had kept her warm before, but now she realized that her fingers were icy and her arms and legs were stiff.

Okay, so what have we got? I'm in a big black *refrigerated* room with a high ceiling and a stone floor. And it's musty and damp.

A cellar? A cellar without windows?

But she was just fooling herself. She knew. The skin of her face seemed to sense the pressure of tons of rock above her. Her ears told her that that musical dripping was water on rock, very far away. Her nose told her that she wasn't in any building. And her fingers could feel the natural irregularity of the ground underneath her.

She didn't want to believe it. But the knowledge crowded in on her, inescapable.

I'm in a cave.

A cave or a cavern. Anyway, I'm *inside* the earth. God knows how deep inside. Deep enough and far enough that I can't see any light from an entrance or vent hole.

Very deep inside, her heart told her.

She was in the loneliest place in the world. And she was going to die here.

Hannah had never had claustrophobia before. But now she couldn't help feeling that the mass of rock around and above her was trying to crush her. It could fall in at any minute, she thought. She felt a physical pressure, as if she were at the bottom of the ocean. She began to have trouble breathing.

She had to get her mind off it. She *refused* to turn into that screaming, gibbering thing in the darkness again. Worse than the thought of dying was the thought of going insane down here.

Think about Thierry. When he finds out you're missing he'll start looking for you. You *know* that. And he won't give up until he finds you.

But I'll be dead by then, she thought involuntarily.

This time, instead of fear, the idea of her death brought a strange poignant loneliness.

Another life where I missed him, she thought. She blinked against tears suddenly. Oh, God. Great.

It's so *hard*. So hard to keep hoping that someday it's going to work out. But I'll meet him again in my next life. And maybe I won't be so stupid then; I won't fall for Maya's tricks.

It'll be harder for him, I guess. He'll have to wait and get through the years day by day. I'll just go to sleep and eventually wake up somewhere else. And then someday he'll come for me and I'll remember . . . and then we'll start all over.

I really did try this time, Thierry. I did my best. I didn't mean to mess things up.

Promise me you'll look for me again.

Promise you'll find me. I promise I'll wait for you.

No matter how long it takes.

Hannah shut her eyes, leaning back against the post and almost unconsciously touching the ring he'd given her. Maybe next time she'd remember it.

Suddenly she didn't feel sad or afraid anymore. Just very tired.

Eyes still shut, she grinned weakly. I feel old. Like Mom's always complaining she feels. Ready to turn this old body in and get a new . . .

The thought broke off and disappeared.

Was that a *noise*?

Hannah found herself sitting up, leaning forward as far as the rope would allow, straining her ears. She thought she'd heard . . . *yes*. There it was again. A solid echoing sound out in the darkness.

It sounded like footsteps. And it was coming closer.

Yes, yes. I'm rescued, I'm saved. Hannah's heart was pounding so hard that she could hardly breathe to yell. But at last, just as she saw a bobbing point of light in the blackness, she managed to get out a hoarse squawk.

"Thierry? Hello? I'm over here!"

The light kept coming toward her. She could hear the footsteps coming closer.

And there was no answer.

"Thierry . . . ?" Her voice trailed off.

Footsteps. The light was big now. It was a beam, a flashlight. Hannah blinked at it.

Her heart was slowly sinking until it seemed to reach stone.

And then the flashlight was right in front of her. It shone in her face, dazzling her eyes. Another light snapped on, a small camping lantern. Vision rushed back to Hannah, sending information surging to her brain.

But there was no happiness in it. Hannah's entire body was ice cold now, shivering.

Because of course it wasn't Thierry. It was Maya.

CHAPTER 15

I hope I didn't disturb you," Maya said.

She put down the lantern and what looked like a black backpack. Then she stood with her hands on her hips and looked at Hannah.

I will not cry. I won't give her the satisfaction, Hannah thought.

"I didn't know vampires could really change into bats," she said.

Maya laughed. She looked beautiful in the pool of lantern light. Her long black hair fell in waves around her, hanging down her back to her hips. Her skin was milky-pale and her eyes looked dark and mysterious. Her laughing mouth was red.

She was wearing designer jeans and high-heeled snakeskin boots. Funny, Hannah had never noticed any of Maya's clothes before. Usually the woman herself was so striking that it was impossible to focus on how she was dressed.

"Not all vampires can shapeshift," Maya said. "But, then, I'm not like other vampires. I'm the first, my darling. I'm the original. And I have to say I'm getting really sick of *you*."

The feeling is mutual, Hannah thought. She said, "Then why don't you leave me alone? Why don't you leave me and Thierry alone?"

"Because, then, my sweet pea, I wouldn't *win*. And I have to win." She looked at Hannah directly, her face oddly serious. "Don't you understand that yet?" she said softly. "I have to win—because I've given up too much to lose. It can't all be for nothing. So winning is all there is."

Hannah's breath was taken away.

She hadn't expected a coherent answer from Maya . . . but she'd gotten one. And she did understand. Maya had devoted her life to keeping Hannah and Thierry apart. Her *long* life. Her thousands of years. If she lost at this point, that life became meaningless.

"You don't know how to do anything else," Hannah whispered slowly, figuring it out.

"Oh, enough of the press conference. I know how to do lots of things—you'll find that out. I'm through fooling around with you, cupcake."

Hannah ignored the threat—and the insulting endearment. "But it won't do you any good," she said, genuinely bewildered, as if she and Maya were discussing whether or not to go shopping together. "You're going to kill me, sure, I understand that.

But it won't help you get Thierry. He'll just hate you more . . . and he'll just wait for me to come back."

Maya had knelt by the backpack, rummaging in it. Now she looked up at Hannah and smiled—a strange slow smile.

"Will he?"

Hannah stared at those red lips, feeling as if someone were pouring ice water down her backbone. "You know he will. Unless you kill him, too."

The lips curved again. "An interesting idea. But not quite what I had in mind. I need him alive; he's my prize, you see. When you win, you need a prize."

Hannah was feeling colder and colder inside. "Then he'll wait."

"Not if you're not coming back."

And how do you arrange *that*? Hannah thought. God, maybe she's going to keep me *alive* here . . . tied up and alive until I'm ninety. The idea brought a wave of suffocating fear. Hannah glanced around, trying to imagine what it would be like to spend her life in this place. In this cold, dark, horrible . . .

Maya burst into laughter.

"You can't figure it out, can you? Well, let me help." She walked to where Hannah was sitting and knelt. "Look at this. Look, Hannah."

She was holding up an oval hand mirror. At the same moment she shone the flashlight on Hannah's face.

Hannah looked into the mirror—and gasped.

It was her face . . . but not her face. For one instant she couldn't put her finger on the difference—all she could think was that it was *Hana's* face, Hana of the Three Rivers. And then she realized.

Her birthmark was gone.

Or . . . *almost* gone. She could still see a shadow of it if she turned her head to one side. But it had faded almost to invisibility.

God, I'm good-looking, Hannah thought numbly. She was too dazed to feel either vain or humble. Then she realized it wasn't just the absence of the birthmark that made her look beautiful.

Even in the unnatural beam of the flashlight she could tell that she was pale. Her skin was creamy, almost translucent. Her eyes seemed larger and brighter. Her mouth seemed softer and more sensuous. And there was an indefinable *something* about her face. . . .

I look like Poppy, she thought. Like Poppy, the girl with the copper hair. The vampire.

Wordlessly, she looked at Maya.

Maya's red lips stretched in a smile.

"Yes. I exchanged blood with you when I picked you up last night. That's why you slept so long . . . you probably don't realize it, but it's afternoon out there. And you're changing already. I figure one more exchange of blood . . . maybe two. I don't want to rush things. I can't have you dying *before* you become a vampire."

Hannah's mind was reeling. Her head fell back weakly to rest against the post. She stared at Maya.

"But *why*?" she whispered, almost pleadingly. "Why make me a vampire?"

Maya stood. She walked over to the backpack and carefully tucked the mirror inside. Then she pulled out something else, something so long that it was sticking out of the top of the pack. She held it up.

A stake. A black wooden stake, like a spear, about as long as Maya's arm. It had a nice pointed end on it.

"Vampires don't come back," Maya said.

Suddenly there was a roaring in Hannah's ears. She swallowed and swallowed. She was afraid she was going to faint or be sick.

"Vampires . . . don't . . . ?"

"It's an interesting bit of trivia, isn't it? Maybe it'll be on *Jeopardy!* someday. I have to admit, I don't exactly understand the logistics—but vampires don't reincarnate, not even if they're Old Souls. They just die. I've heard it suggested that it's because making them vampires takes their souls away, but I don't know. . . . Does Thierry have a soul, do you think?"

Everything was whirling around Hannah now. There was nothing solid, nothing to hang on to.

To die . . . she could face that. But to die forever, to go *out* . . . what if vampires didn't even go to some other place, some afterlife? What if they just suddenly *weren't*?

It was the most frightening thing she had ever imagined.

"I won't let you," she whispered, hearing her own voice come out hoarse and ragged. "I won't—"

"But you can't stop me," Maya said, amused. "Those ropes are hemp—they'll hold you when you're a vampire as well as when you're human. You're helpless, poor baby. You can't do anything against me." With a look of pleasure in her own cleverness, she said, "I finally found a way to break the cycle."

She left the backpack and knelt in front of Hannah again. This time when the red lips parted, Hannah saw long sharp teeth.

Hannah fought. Even knowing that it was hopeless, she did everything she could think of, lashing out at Maya with the strength of sheer desperation. But it wasn't any good. Maya was simply that much stronger than she was. In a matter of minutes, Hannah found herself with both hands pinned and her head twisted to one side, her throat exposed.

Now she knew why Maya had forced her to drink vampire blood before. It hadn't just been random cruelty. It was part of a plan.

You can't do this to me. You *can't*. You can't kill my soul. . . .

"Ready or not," Maya said, almost humming it.

Then Hannah felt teeth.

She struggled again, like a gazelle in the jaws of a lioness. It had no effect. She could feel the unique pain of her blood being drawn out against her will. She could feel Maya drinking deeply.

I don't want this to be happening. . . .

At last the pain faded to a drowsy sort of ache. Hannah's mind felt dopey, her body numb.

Maya was wrestling her into a different position, tilting Hannah's head back and pressing her wrist to Hannah's mouth.

I won't drink. I'll let myself drown first. At least I'll die before I'm a vampire. . . .

But she found that it wasn't that easy to will yourself into dying from lack of air. Eventually, she choked and swallowed Maya's blood. She wound up coughing and sputtering, trying to clear her throat and get air.

Maya sat back.

"There," she said, slightly breathless. She shone the flashlight into Hannah's face again.

"Yes." She looked judicial, like a woman considering a turkey in the oven. "Yes, it's going very well. Once more should do it. You'd be a vampire now, if we hadn't wasted so much time since the first exchange."

"Thierry will kill you when he finds out," Hannah whispered.

"And break his sacred promise? I don't *think* so." Maya smiled and got up again, pottering with her backpack. "Of course, this wouldn't be happening if he hadn't broken his promise to *me*," she added, almost matter-of-factly. "He told me that you wouldn't come between us anymore. But the next time I turn around—there you are! Shacked up in his house, no less. He should have known better."

Hannah stared at her. "He didn't even know I was there. Maya—don't you realize that? He didn't know—"

Maya cut her off with a gesture. "Don't expect me to believe anything you say. Not at this point." She straightened up, looked at Hannah, then sighed. She switched off the lantern and picked up the flashlight. "I'm afraid I'm going to have to leave you for a while, now. I'll be back tonight to finish this little job. Don't worry, I won't be late . . . after all, I have a deadline to meet. Tomorrow's your birthday."

"Maya . . ." I have to keep her here talking, Hannah thought. I have to make her understand that Thierry didn't break his promise.

She was trying to ignore the chilling question that ran just under her thoughts. What if Thierry had been serious about what he'd told Maya? If he really wanted to be with Maya as long as Hannah was no longer between them?

"Can't stay; must fly," Maya said, trilling laughter again. "I hope you won't be too lonely. By the way, I wouldn't rock that pole too much. This is an abandoned silver mine, and that whole structure is unstable."

"Maya—"

"See you later." She picked up the backpack and walked away.

She ignored Hannah's yells. And eventually, when Hannah couldn't see the beam of the flashlight anymore, she stopped yelling.

She was in the dark again.

And weaker. Drained emotionally and drained of vitality by what Maya had done. She felt sick, feverish, and itchy as if there were bugs crawling under her skin.

And she was alone.

Almost, *almost*, she gave in to the panic again. But she was afraid that if she lost control this time, she'd never get it back. She'd be insane by the time Maya returned.

Time. That's it, girl, you've got some time. She's not coming back until tonight, so get your head clear and start using the time you have.

But it's so dark. . . .

Wait. Did she take the lantern with her? She turned it off, but did she *take* it?

With the utmost caution, Hannah felt around her with her hands. Nothing—but then she couldn't lean very far because of the rope.

Okay. Try your feet. *Carefully.* If you kick it away, it's all over.

Hannah lifted one leg and began to gently pat the foot down toward the ground. Little pats, slow pats. About the third time she did it, her foot hit something that fell over.

That's it! Now nudge it toward you. Careful. Careful.

Closer . . . almost . . . now around to your side . . .

Got it! Hannah reached out and grabbed the lantern, holding it desperately with both hands like somebody holding a radio while sitting in the bathtub. Don't drop it . . . find the switch.

Light blossomed.

Hannah kissed the lantern. She actually kissed it. It was an ordinary battery-operated fluorescent camping lantern, but she felt as if she were holding a miracle.

Light made such a difference.

Okay. Now look around you. What can you do to help yourself here?

But looking around made her heart sink.

The cavern she was in was irregular, with uneven walls and overhanging slabs of rock. A silver mine, Maya had said. That meant the place was probably blasted out by humans.

On either side of her, Hannah could see more posts like the one she was tied to. They seemed to form a kind of scaffolding against the wall. So miners can get to it, I guess, she thought vaguely. Or maybe to help hold the roof up, or both.

And it's unstable.

As a last resort, she could simply do her best to bring the whole thing down. And then pray she died quickly.

For now, she kept looking.

The wall on her right, the only one she could see in the pool of lantern light, was surprisingly variegated. Even beautiful. It wasn't just rough gray rock; it was rough gray rock veined with milky-white and pale pink quartz.

Silver comes in quartz sometimes, Hannah thought. She knew that much from her mom's friends, the rockhounds.

But that doesn't do me any good. It's pretty, but useless.

She was starting to panic again. She had a light, but what good was it? She could see, but she had nothing to work with.

There's got to be *something* here. Rocks. I've got rocks and that's it. Hannah shifted to get away from one that was bruising her thigh. Maybe I can throw rocks at her. . . .

Not rocks. Quartz.

Suddenly Hannah's whole body was tingling. Her breath was stopped in her lungs and her skin felt electrified.

I've got quartz.

With shaking hands, she put the lantern down. She reached for an angular chunk of rock on the ground beside her.

Tears sprang to her eyes.

This is a quartz nodule. It's crystal. Fine-grained. Workable.

I know how to make a tool out of this.

She'd never done it in this life, of course. But Hana of the Three Rivers had done it all the time. She'd made knives, scrapers, drills . . . and hand-axes.

She would have preferred flint to work with; it fractured much more regularly. But quartz was fine.

I can feel in my hands how to do it. . . .

Okay. Stay calm. First, find a hammer stone.

It was too easy. There were rocks all around her. Hannah picked up one with a slightly rounded surface, weighed it in her hand. It felt good.

She pulled her legs in, set the angular chunk in front of her, and started working.

She didn't actually make a hand-ax. She didn't need to. Once she had bashed off a few flakes with long sharp edges, she started sawing at the rope. The flakes were wavy and irregular, but they were as sharp as broken glass and quite sufficient to cut the hemp.

It took a long time, and twice she had to make new flakes when the ones she was using blunted. But she was patient. She kept working until she could pull first one length of rope, then another and another free.

When the last strand parted, she almost screamed in sheer joy.

I'm free! I did it! I did it!

She jumped up, her weakness and fever forgotten. She danced around the room. Then she ran back and picked up her precious lantern.

And now—I'm out of here!

But she wasn't.

It took a while for the realization to dawn. First, she walked back in the direction that Maya had come. She found what felt like miles of twisting passageways, sometimes so narrow that the walls almost brushed her shoulders, and so low that she had to duck her head. The rock was cold—and wet.

There were several branching passages, but each one led to a dead end. And it was only when Hannah got to the end of the main passage that she realized how Maya had gotten into the mine.

She was standing below a vertical shaft. It soared maybe a hundred feet straight up. At the very top, she could see reddish sunlight.

It was like a giant chimney, except that the walls were nowhere near that close to each other. And nowhere near irregular enough to climb.

No human could get out this way.

I suppose they had some sort of elevator or something when the mine was working, Hannah thought dazedly. She was sick and numb. She couldn't believe that her triumph had turned into this.

For a while she shouted, staring up at that square of infuriating, unattainable sunlight. When she got so hoarse she could scarcely hear herself anymore, she admitted that it was no use.

Nobody is going to come and rescue you. Okay. So you have to rescue yourself.

But all I've got is rocks. . . . No.

No, I'm free now. I can move around. I can get to the scaffolding.

I've got rocks—and wood.

SOULMATE

Hannah stood paralyzed for a second, then she clutched the lantern to her chest and went running back down the passageway.

When she got to her cavern, she examined the scaffolding excitedly.

Yes. Some of this wood is still good. It's old, but it's hard. I can work with this.

This time, she made a real hand-ax, taking special care to fashion the tip, making it thin and straight-edged and sharp. The final tool was roughly triangular and heavy. It fit comfortably in her hand. Hana would have been proud of it.

Then she used the ax to chop off a length of wood from the creaking, groaning scaffolding. All the while she did it she whistled softly, hoping she wasn't going to bring the whole structure down on her head.

She used the ax to shape the length of wood, too, making it round, about as thick as her thumb and as long as her forearm. She knocked off a quartz scraper to do the finer shaping.

Finally she used a flake to hone one end of the stick to a point. She ground it back and forth against an outcrop of gritty stone to bring it to maximum smoothness and sharpness.

Then she held out the finished tool and admired it.

She had a stake. A very good stake.

And Maya was going to get a surprise.

Hannah sat down, turned the lantern off to conserve the battery, and began to wait.

CHAPTER 16

It was a very long time before Hannah heard footsteps again.

She distracted herself during the long wait by whistling songs under her breath and thinking about the people she loved.

Her mother. Her mother didn't even miss her yet, didn't know she was gone. But by tomorrow she would. Tomorrow was May first, Hannah's birthday, and Chess would give her mother the letter.

Chess, of course. Hannah wished now that she'd spent more time saying goodbye to Chess, that she'd explained things better. Chess would have been fascinated. And she had a right to know she was an Old Soul, too.

Paul Winfield. That was strange—she'd only known him a week. But he'd tried to help her. And at this moment, he knew more about Hannah Snow than anyone else in Montana.

I hope he doesn't start smoking again if he finds out I'm dead.

Because that was probably how she would end up. Hannah had no illusions about that. She had a weapon—but so did Maya, and Maya was much faster and stronger. She was no match for Maya under the best of circumstances, much less when she was weak and feverish. The best she could hope for was to get Maya to kill her while she was still human.

She thought about the Circle Daybreak members. They were good people. She was sorry she wouldn't have the chance to know them better, to help them. They were doing something important, something she instinctively sensed was necessary right now.

And she thought about Thierry.

He'll have to go wandering again, I guess. It's too bad. He hasn't had a very happy life. I was starting to think I could take that sadness out of his eyes. . . .

When she heard a noise at last, she thought it might be her imagination. She held her breath.

No. It's footsteps. Getting closer.

She's coming.

Hannah shifted position. She had stationed herself near the mouth of the cavern; now she took a deep breath and eased herself into a crouch. She wiped her sweaty right palm on her jeans and got a better grip on her stake.

She figured that Maya would shine the flashlight toward the

pole where Hannah had been tied, then maybe take a few steps farther inside the cavern, trying to see what was going on.

And then I'll do it. I'll come out of the darkness behind her. Jump and skewer her through the back. But I've got to time it right.

She held her breath as she saw light outside the mouth of the cavern. Her greatest fear was that Maya would *hear* her.

Quiet . . . quiet . . .

The light came closer. Hannah watched it, not moving. But her brain was clicking along in surprise. It wasn't the slanted, focused beam of a flashlight. It was the more diffuse pool of light from a lantern.

She's brought another one. But that means . . .

Maya was walking in.

Walking quickly—and not pausing. She couldn't shine the light onto the pole yet. And she didn't seem anxious to— apparently it didn't occur to her that she needed to check on Hannah. She was that confident.

Hannah cursed mentally. She's going too far—she's out of range. Get up!

Her plan in ruins, she flexed her knees and stood. She heard a crack in her knee joint that sounded as loud as a gunshot.

But Maya didn't stop. She kept going. She was almost at the pole.

As silently as she could, Hannah headed across the cavern. All Maya had to do was turn around to see her.

Maya was at the pole. She was stopping. She was looking from side to side.

Hannah was behind her.

Now.

Now was the time. Hannah's muscles could feel how she had to stab, to throw her weight behind the thrust so that the stake went in under Maya's left shoulder blade. She knew how to do it. . . .

But she couldn't.

She couldn't stab somebody in the back. Somebody who wasn't menacing her at the moment, who didn't even know they were in danger.

Oh, my God! Don't be stupid! *Do* it!

Oh, my Goddess! a voice echoed back in her head. You're not a killer. This isn't even self-defense!

Frustrated almost to the point of hysteria, Hannah heard herself let out a breath. It was wet. She was crying.

Her arm drooped. Her muscles collapsed. She wasn't doing it. She couldn't do it.

Maya slowly turned around.

She looked both beautiful and eerie in the lantern light. She surveyed Hannah up and down, looking in particular at the drooping stake.

Then she looked at Hannah's face.

"You're the strangest girl," she said, in what seemed to be genuine bewilderment. "Why didn't you do it? You were smart enough to get yourself out and make yourself a weapon. Why didn't you have the guts to finish it?"

Hannah was asking herself the same thing. Only with more expletives.

I am going to die now, she thought. And maybe die for good—because I don't have guts. Because I couldn't kill somebody I know is completely evil and completely determined to kill me.

That's not ethics. That's *stupid*.

"I suppose it's that Egyptian temple training," Maya was saying. "Or maybe the life when you were a Buddhist—do you remember that? Or maybe you're just weak."

And a victim. I've spent a couple thousand years being a victim—yours. I guess I've got my part down perfect by now.

"Oh, well. It doesn't really matter why," Maya said. "It all comes down to the same thing in the end. Now. Let's get this over with."

Hannah stared at her, breathing hard, feeling like a rabbit looking at a headlight.

Nobody should live as a victim. Every creature has a right to fight for its life.

But she couldn't seem to get her muscles to move anymore. She was just too tired. Every part of her hurt, from her throbbing head to her raw fingertips to her bruised and aching feet.

Maya was smiling, fixing her with eyes that shifted from lapis-lazuli blue to glacier green.

"Be a good girl, now," she crooned.

I don't want to be a good girl. . . .

Maya reached for her with long arms.

"Don't touch her!" Thierry said from the cavern mouth.

Hannah's head jerked sideways. She stared at the new pool of light on the other side of the cave. For the first few seconds she thought she was hallucinating.

But, no. He was there. Thierry was standing there with a lantern of his own, tall and almost shimmering with coiled tension, like a predator ready to spring.

The problem was that he was too far away. And Maya was too fast. In the same instant that it took Hannah to make her brain believe her eyes, Maya was moving. In one swift step, she was behind Hannah, with her hands around Hannah's throat.

"Stay where you are," she said. "Or I'll break her little neck."

Hannah knew she could do it. She could feel the iron strength in Maya's hands. Maya didn't need a weapon.

Thierry put the lantern down and raised his empty hands. "I'm staying," he said quietly.

"And tell whoever else you've got in that tunnel to go back. All the way back. If I see another person, I'll kill her."

Without turning, Thierry shouted. "Go back to the entrance. All of you." Then he looked at Hannah. "Are you all right?"

Hannah couldn't nod. Maya's grip was so tight that she could barely say, "Yes." But she could look at him, and she could see his eyes.

She knew, in that moment, that all her fears about him not wanting her anymore were groundless. He loved her. She had never seen such open love and concern in anyone's face before.

More, they *understood* each other. They didn't need any words. It was the end of misunderstandings and mistrust. For perhaps the first time since she had been Hana of the Three Rivers, Hannah trusted him without reservation.

They were in accord.

And neither of them wanted this to end with a death.

When Thierry took his eyes from Hannah's, it was to look at Maya and say, "It's over, now. You have to realize that. I've got twenty people down here, and another twenty on the surface waiting." His voice became softer and more deliberate. "But I give you my word, you can walk out of here right now, Maya. Nobody will touch you. All you have to do is let Hannah go first."

"Together," Hannah said, coughing as Maya's hands tightened, cutting off her breath. She gasped and finished, "We go out together, Thierry."

Thierry nodded and looked at Maya. He was holding his hand out now, like someone trying to coax a frightened child. "Just let her go," he said softly.

Maya laughed.

It was an unnatural sound, and it made Hannah's skin crawl. Nothing sane made a noise like that.

"But that way, I won't *win*," Maya said, almost pleasantly.

"You can't win anyway," Thierry said quietly. "Even if you kill her, she'll still be alive—"

"Not if I make her a vampire first," Maya interrupted.

But Thierry was shaking his head. "It doesn't matter." His voice was still quiet, but it was filled with the authority of absolute conviction, a kind of bedrock certainty that held even Hannah mesmerized.

"Even if you kill her, she'll still be alive—here." He tapped his chest. "In me. I keep her here. She's *part* of me. So until you kill me, you can't really kill her. And you can't win. It's that simple."

There was a silence. Hannah's own heart was twisted with the force of her love for him. Her eyes were full.

She could hear Maya breathing, and the sound was ragged. She thought that the pressure of Maya's hands was infinitesimally less.

"I could kill you both," Maya said at last in a grating voice.

Thierry lifted his shoulders and dropped them in a gesture too sad to be a shrug. "But how can you win when the people you hate aren't there to see it?"

It sounded insane—but it was true. Hannah could feel it hit Maya like a well-thrown javelin. If Maya couldn't have Thierry as her prize, if she couldn't even make him suffer, what was the point? Where was the victory?

"Let's stop the cycle right here," Thierry said softly. "Let her go."

He was so gentle, and so reasonable, and so tired-sounding. Hannah didn't see how anyone could resist him. But she was still surprised at what happened next.

Slowly, very slowly, the hands around her neck loosened their grip. Maya stepped away.

Hannah sucked in a deep breath. She wanted to run to Thierry, but she was afraid to do anything to unbalance the delicate stalemate in the cavern. Besides, her knees were wobbly.

Maya was moving around her, taking a step or two in front of her, facing Thierry directly.

"I loved you," she said. There was a sound in her voice Hannah had never heard before, a quaver. "Why didn't you ever understand that?"

Thierry shook his head. "Because it's not true. You never loved me. You wanted me. Mostly because you couldn't have me."

There was a silence then as they stood looking at each other. Not because they understood each other too well for words, Hannah thought. Because they would never understand each other. They had nothing to say.

The silence stretched on and on—and then Maya collapsed.

She didn't fall down. But she might as well have. Hannah saw the life go out of her—the *hope*. The energy that had kept Maya vibrant and sparkling after thousands of years. It had all come from her need to win . . . and now she knew she'd lost.

She was defeated.

"Come on, Hannah," Thierry said quietly. "Let's go." Then he turned to shout back into the tunnel behind him. "Clear the way. We're all coming out."

That was when it happened.

Maya had been standing slumped, her head down, her eyes on the ground.

Or on her backpack.

And now, as Thierry turned away, she flashed one glance at him and then moved as fast as a striking snake. She grabbed the black stake and held it horizontally, her arm drawn back.

Hannah recognized the posture instantly. As Hana of the Three Rivers she'd seen hunters throw spears all the time.

"Game over," Maya whispered.

Hannah had a fraction of a second to act—and no time to consider. All she thought was, *No.*

With her whole weight behind the thrust, she lunged at Maya. Stake first.

The sharp wooden point went in just under Maya's shoulder blade. She staggered, off balance, her throw ruined. The black stake went skittering across the rough stone floor.

Hannah was off balance, too. She was falling. Maya was falling. But it all seemed to be happening in slow motion.

I've killed her.

There was no triumph in the thought. Only a sort of hushed certainty.

When the slow-motion feeling ended, she found herself the way anybody finds themself after a fall. On the ground and surprised. Except that Maya was underneath her, with a stake protruding from her back.

Hannah's first frantic thought was to get a doctor. She'd never seen someone this badly hurt before—not in this life. There was blood seeping out of Maya's back around the make-shift stake. It had gone in very deep, the wood piercing vampire flesh like razor-sharp steel through a human.

Thierry was beside her. Kneeling, pulling Hannah slightly away from Maya's prone form, as if she might still be dangerous.

Hannah reached for him at the same time, and their hands met, intertwined. She held on tight, feeling a rush of warmth and comfort from his presence.

Then Thierry gently turned Maya onto her side.

Hair was falling across Maya's face like a black waterfall. Her skin was chalky white and her eyes were wide open. But she was laughing.

Laughing.

She looked at Hannah and laughed. In a thick choking voice, she gasped. "You had guts—after all."

Hannah whispered, "Can we do anything for her?"

Thierry shook his head.

Then it was terrible. Maya's laugh turned into a gurgle. A trickle of blood ran out of the side of her mouth. Her body jerked. Her eyes stared. And then, finally, she was still.

Hannah felt her own breath sigh out.

She's dead. I killed her. I killed someone.

Every creature has the right to fight for its life—or its loved ones.

Thierry said softly, "The cycle is broken."

Then he let Maya's shoulder go and her body slumped down again. She seemed smaller now, shrunken. After a moment Hannah realized it wasn't an illusion. Maya was doing what all vampires do in the movies. She was falling in on herself, her tissues collapsing, muscle and flesh shriveling. The one hand Hannah could see seemed to be wasting away and hardening at the same time. The skin became yellow and leathery, showing the form of the tendons underneath.

In the end, Maya was just a leather sack full of bones.

Hannah swallowed and shut her eyes.

"Are you all right? Let me look at you." Thierry was holding her, examining her. Then when Hannah met his eyes, he looked at her long and searchingly and said with a different meaning, "Are you all right?"

Hannah understood. She looked at Maya and then back at him.

"I'm not proud of it," she said slowly. "But I'm not sorry, either. It just—had to be done." She thought another moment, then said, getting out each word separately, "I refuse to be . . . a victim . . . anymore."

Thierry tightened his arm around her. "*I'm* proud of you,"

he said. Then he added, "Let's go. We need to get you to a healer."

They walked back through the narrow passageway, which was no longer dark because Thierry's people had placed lanterns every few feet. At the end of the passage, in the room with the vertical shaft, they had set up some sort of rope and pulley.

Lupe was there, and Nilsson, and the rest of the CIA group. So were Rashel and Quinn. The fighters, Hannah thought. Everyone called and laughed and patted her when she came in with Thierry.

"It's over," Thierry said briefly. "She's dead."

Everyone looked at him and then at Hannah. And somehow they knew. They all cheered and patted her again. Hannah didn't feel like Cinderella anymore; she felt like Dorothy after killing the Wicked Witch.

And she didn't like it.

Lupe took her by the shoulders and said excitedly, "Do you know what you've done?"

Hannah said, "Yes. But I don't want to think about it any more right now."

It wasn't until they'd hauled her up the vertical shaft that it occurred to her to ask Thierry how he'd found her. She was standing on an inconspicuous hillside with no buildings or landmarks around. Maya had picked a very good hiding place.

"One of her own people sold her out," Thierry said. "He got to the house about the same time I did this evening, and he said he had information to sell. He was a werewolf who wasn't happy with how she'd treated him."

A werewolf with black hair? Hannah wondered. But she was too sleepy suddenly to ask more questions.

"Home, sir?" Nilsson said, a little breathlessly because he'd just come up the shaft.

Thierry looked at him, laughed, and started to help Hannah down the hill. "That's right. Home, Nilsson."

CHAPTER 17

I need to call my mom," Hannah said.

Thierry nodded. "But maybe wait until she's up. It's not dawn yet."

They were at Thierry's house, in the elegant bedroom with the softly burnished gold walls. The window had just begun to turn gray.

It was so good to rest, to let go of tension, to feel her battered body relax. It was so good to be *alive*. She felt as if she'd been reborn and was looking at the world with wide new eyes. Even the smallest comforts—a hot drink, a fire in the fireplace—were immeasurably precious.

And it was good to be with Thierry.

He was sitting on the bed, holding her hand, watching her as if he couldn't believe she was real.

The healer had come and gone, and now it was just the two of them. They sat together quietly, not needing words.

They looked into each other's eyes, and then they were reaching for each other, holding each other. Resting like weary travelers in each other's arms.

Hannah leaned her forehead against Thierry's lips.

It's over, she thought. I was right when I told Paul the apocalypse was coming—but it's over now.

Thierry stirred, kissing the hair on her forehead. Then he spoke, not out loud but with his mental voice. As soon as Hannah heard it, she knew he was trying to say something serious and important.

You know, you came very close to becoming a vampire. You're going to be sick for a few days while your body shifts back to human.

Hannah nodded without pulling away to look at him. The healer had told her all that. She sensed that there was something more Thierry wanted to say.

And . . . well, you still have a choice, you know.

There was a silence. Then Hannah did pull away to look at him. "What do you mean?"

He took a deep breath, then said out loud, "I mean, you can still choose to be a vampire. You're right on the edge. If you want, we can make you change over."

Hannah took a long breath of her own.

She hadn't thought about this—but she was thinking now. As a vampire, she'd be immortal; she could stay with Thierry continuously for who knew how many thousands of years? She would be stronger than a human, faster, telepathic.

And perfect physically. Involuntarily, her hand went to her left cheek, to her birthmark.

The doctors couldn't take it away. But becoming a vampire would.

She looked directly at Thierry. "Is that what you want? For me to become a vampire?"

He was looking at her cheek, too. Then he met her eyes.

"I want what *you* want. I want you to be happy. Nothing else matters to me."

Hannah took her hand away.

"Then," she said very softly, "if you don't mind, I'll stay human. I don't mind the birthmark. It's just—part of me, now. It doesn't bring up any bad memories." After a moment, she added, "All humans are imperfect, I guess."

She could see tears in Thierry's eyes. He gently lifted her hand and kissed it. He didn't say anything, but something about his expression made Hannah's throat and chest fill with love.

Then he took her in his arms.

And Hannah was happy. So happy that she was crying a little, too.

She was with her flying companion—her playmate. The one who was sacred to her, who was the other half of the mysteries of life for her. The one who would always be there for her, helping her, watching her back, picking her up when she fell down, listening to her stories—no matter how many times she told them. Loving her even when she was stupid. Understanding her without words. Being inside the innermost circle in her mind.

Her soulmate.

Things are going to be all right now, she thought.

Suddenly it was as if she could see the corridor of time again, but this time looking forward, not back.

She would go to college and become a paleontologist. And she and Thierry would work with Circle Daybreak and the Old Powers that were rising. They would be happy together, and they would help the world through the enormous changes that were coming.

The sadness would go out of Thierry's eyes.

They would love and discover and learn and explore. And Hannah would grow up and get older, and Thierry would love her just the same. And then one day, being human, she would go back to Mother Earth, like a wave going out to the ocean. Thierry would grieve for her—and wait for her.

And then they would start all over again.

One lifetime with him was enough, but Hannah sensed that there would be many. There would always be something new to learn.

Thierry moved, his breath warming her hair. "I almost forgot," he whispered. "You're seventeen today. Congratulations."

That's right, Hannah thought. She looked toward the window, startled and overwhelmed. The sky was turning pink

now. She was seeing the dawn of her seventeenth birthday—
something that had never happened before.

I've changed my destiny.

"I love you," she whispered to Thierry.

And then they just sat together, holding each other as the
room filled with light.

The Night World
lives on in *Huntress*,
by L. J. Smith.

I t's simple," Jez said on the night of the last hunt of her life.
"You run. We chase. If we catch you, you die. We'll give
you three minutes' head start."

The skinhead gang leader in front of her didn't move. He had
a pasty face and shark eyes. He was standing tensely, trying to look
tough, but Jez could see the little quiver in his leg muscles.

Jez flashed him a smile.

"Pick a weapon," she said. Her toe nudged the pile at her
feet. There was a lot of stuff there—guns, knives, baseball bats,
even a few spears. "Hey, take *more* than one. Take as many as
you want. My treat."

There was a stifled giggle from behind her and Jez made a
sharp gesture to stop it. Then there was silence. The two gangs
stood facing each other, six skinhead thugs on one side and
Jez's gang on the other. Except that Jez's people weren't exactly
normal gang members.

The skinhead leader's eyes shifted to the pile. Then he made a sudden lunge and came up with something in his hand.

A gun, of course. They always picked guns. This particular gun was the kind it was illegal to buy in California these days, a large caliber semiautomatic assault weapon. The skinhead whipped it up and held it pointed straight at Jez.

Jez threw back her head and laughed.

Everyone was staring at her—and that was fine. She looked great and she knew it.

Hands on her hips, red hair tumbling over her shoulders and down her back, fine-boned face tipped to the sky—yeah, she looked good. Tall and proud and fierce . . . and very beautiful. She was Jez Redfern, the huntress.

She lowered her chin and fixed the gang leader with eyes that were neither silver nor blue but some color in between. A color he never could have seen before, because no human had eyes like that.

He didn't get the clue. He didn't seem like the brightest.

"Chase this," he said, and he fired the gun.

Jez moved at the last instant. Not that metal through the chest would have seriously hurt her, but it might have knocked her backward and she didn't want that. She'd just taken over the leadership of the gang from Morgead, and she didn't want to show any weakness.

The bullet passed through her left arm. There was a little explosion of blood and a sharp flash of pain as it fractured the bone before passing on through. Jez narrowed her eyes, but held on to her smile.

Then she glanced down at her arm and lost the smile, hissing. She hadn't considered the damage to her sleeve. Now there was a bloody hole in it. Why didn't she ever think about these things?

"Do you know how much leather costs? Do you know how much a North Beach jacket costs?" She advanced on the skinhead leader.

He was blinking and hyperventilating. Trying to figure out how she'd moved so fast and why she wasn't yelling in agony. He aimed the gun and fired again. And again, each time more wildly.

Jez dodged. She didn't want any more holes. The flesh of her arm was already healing, closing up and smoothing over. Too bad her jacket couldn't do the same. She reached the skinhead without getting hit again and grabbed him by the front of his green and black Air Force flight jacket. She lifted him, one-handed, until the steel toes of his Doc Marten boots just cleared the ground.

"You better run, boy," she said. Then she threw him.

He sailed through the air a remarkable distance and bounced off a tree. He scrambled up, his eyes showing white with terror, his chest heaving. He looked at her, looked at his gang, then turned and started running through the redwoods.

The other gang members stared after him for a moment

before diving for the weapons pile. Jez watched them, frowning. They'd just seen how effective bullets were against people like her, but they still went for the guns, passing by perfectly good split-bamboo knives, yew arrows, and a gorgeous snakewood walking stick.

And then things were noisy for a while as the skinheads came up from the pile and started firing. Jez's gang dodged easily, but an exasperated voice sounded in Jez's head.

Can we go after them now? Or do you want to show off some more?

She flicked a glance behind her. Morgead Blackthorn was seventeen, a year older than she, and her worst enemy. He was conceited, hotheaded, stubborn, and power-hungry—and it didn't help that he was always saying she was all those things, too.

"I told them three minutes," she said out loud. "You want me to break my word?" And for that instant, while she was snarling at him, she forgot to keep track of bullets.

The next thing she knew Morgead was knocking her backward. He was lying on top of her. Something whizzed over both of them and hit a tree, spraying bark.

Morgead's gem-green eyes glared down into hers. "But . . . they're . . . not . . . running," he said with exaggerated patience. "In case you hadn't noticed."

He was too close. His hands were on either side of her head. His weight was on her. Jez kicked him off, furious with him and appalled at herself.

"This is *my* game. *I* thought of it. We play it my way!" she yelled.

The skinheads were scattering anyway. They'd finally realized that shooting was pointless. They were running, crashing through the sword fern.

"Okay, now!" Jez said. "But the leader's mine."

There was a chorus of shouts and hunting calls from her gang. Val, the biggest and always the most impatient, dashed off first, yelling something like "Yeeeeeehaw." Then Thistle and Raven went, the slight blonde and the tall dark girl sticking together as always. Pierce hung back, staring with his cold eyes at a tree, waiting to give his prey the illusion of escaping.

Jez didn't look to see what Morgead was doing. Why should she care?

She started off in the direction the skinhead leader had taken. But she didn't exactly take his path. She went through the trees, jumping from one redwood to another. The giant sequoias were the best; they had the thickest branches, although the wartlike bulges called burls on the coastal redwoods were good landing places, too. Jez jumped and grabbed and jumped again, occasionally doing acrobatic flips when she caught a branch just for the fun of it.

She loved Muir Woods. Even though all the wood around her was deadly—or maybe because it was. She liked taking risks. And the place was beautiful: the cathedral silence, the mossy greenness, the resinous smell.

Last week they'd hunted seven gang members through Golden Gate Park. It had been enjoyable, but not really private, and they couldn't let the humans fight back much. Gunshots in the park would attract attention. Muir Woods had been Jez's idea—they could kidnap the gang members and bring them here where nobody would disturb them. They would give them weapons. It would be a real hunt, with real danger.

Jez squatted on a branch to catch her breath. There just wasn't enough real danger in the world, she thought. Not like the old days, when there were still vampire hunters left in the Bay Area. Jez's parents had been killed by vampire hunters. But now that they'd all been eliminated, there wasn't anything really scary anymore. . . .

She froze. There was an almost inaudible crunching in the pine needles ahead of her. Instantly she was on the move again, leaping fearlessly off the branch into space, landing on the spongy pine-needle carpet with her knees bent. She turned and stood face-to-face with the skinhead.

"Hey there," she said.

The skinhead's face was contorted, his eyes huge. He stared at her, breathing hard like a hurt animal.

"I know," Jez said. "You ran fast. You can't figure out how I ran faster."

"You're—not—human," the skinhead panted. Except that he threw in a lot of other words, the kind humans liked to use when they were upset.

"You guessed," Jez said cheerfully, ignoring the obscenities. "You're not as dumb as you look."

"What—the hell—are you?"

"Death." Jez smiled at him. "Are you going to fight? I hope so."

He fumbled the gun up again. His hands were shaking so hard he could scarcely aim it.

"I think you're out of ammo," Jez said. "But anyway a branch would be better. You want me to break one off for you?"

He pulled the trigger. The gun just clicked. He looked at it. Jez smiled at him, showing her teeth.

She could feel them grow as she went into feeding mode. Her canines lengthening and curving until they were as sharp and delicate and translucent as a cat's. She liked the feel of them lightly indenting her lower lip as she half-opened her mouth.

That wasn't the only change. She knew that her eyes were turning to liquid silver and her lips were getting redder and fuller as blood flowed into them in anticipation of feeding. Her whole body was taking on an indefinable charge of energy.

The skinhead watched as she became more and more beautiful, more and more inhuman. And then he seemed to fold in on himself. With his back against a tree, he slid down until he was sitting on the ground in the middle of some pale brown oyster fungus. He was staring straight ahead.

Jez's gaze was drawn to the double lightning bolt tattooed on his neck. Right . . . there, she thought. The skin seemed reasonably clean, and the smell of blood was enticing. It was running there, rich with adrenaline, in blue veins just under the surface. She was almost intoxicated just thinking about tapping it.

Fear was good; it added that extra spice to the taste. Like SweeTarts. This was going to be good. . . .

Then she heard a soft broken sound.

The skinhead was crying.

Not loud bawling. Not blubbering and begging. Just crying like a kid, slow tears trickling down his cheeks as he shook.

"I thought better of you," Jez said. She shook her hair out, tossed it in contempt. But something inside her seemed to tighten.

He didn't say anything. He just stared at her—no, *through* her—and cried. Jez knew what he was seeing. His own death.

"Oh, come on," Jez said. "So you don't want to die. Who does? But you've killed people before. Your gang killed that guy Juan last week. You can dish it out, but you can't take it."

He still didn't say anything. He wasn't pointing the gun at her anymore; he was clutching it with both hands to his chest as if it were a teddy bear or something. Or maybe as if he were going to kill himself to get away from her. The muzzle of the gun was under his chin.

The thing inside Jez tightened more. Tightened and twisted until she couldn't breathe. What was wrong with her? He was just a human, and a human of the worst kind. He *deserved* to die, and not just because she was hungry.

But the sound of that crying . . . It seemed to pull at her. She had a feeling almost of déjà vu, as if this had all happened before—but it *hadn't*. She knew it hadn't.

The skinhead spoke at last. "Do it quick," he whispered.

And Jez's mind was thrown into chaos.

With just those words she was suddenly not in the forest anymore. She was falling into nothingness, whirling and spinning, with nothing to grab hold of. She saw pictures in bright, disjointed flashes. Nothing made sense; she was plunging in darkness with scenes unreeling before her helpless eyes.

"Do it quickly," somebody whispered. A flash and Jez saw who: a woman with dark red hair and delicate, bony shoulders. She had a face like a medieval princess. "I won't fight you," the woman said. "Kill me. But let my daughter live."

Mother . . .

These were her memories.

She wanted to see more of her mother—she didn't have any conscious memory of the woman who'd given birth to her. But instead there was another flash. A little girl was huddled in a corner, shaking. The child had flame-bright hair and eyes that were neither silver nor blue. And she was so frightened . . .

Another flash. A tall man running to the child. Turning around, standing in front of her. "Leave her alone! It's not her fault. She doesn't have to die!"

Daddy.

Her parents, who'd been killed when she was four. Executed by vampire hunters. . . .

Another flash and she saw fighting. Blood. Dark figures struggling with her mother and father. And screaming that wouldn't quite resolve into words.

And then one of the dark figures picked up the little girl in the corner and held her up high . . . and Jez saw that he had fangs. He wasn't a vampire hunter; he was a vampire.

And the little girl, whose mouth was open in a wail, had none.

All at once, Jez could understand the screaming.

"Kill her! Kill the human! Kill the freak!"

They were screaming it about *her*.

Jez came back to herself. She was in Muir Woods, kneeling in the ferns and moss, with the skinhead cowering in front of her. Everything was the same . . . but everything was different. She felt dazed and terrified.

What did it *mean*?

It was just some bizarre hallucination. It had to be. She knew how her parents had died. Her mother had been murdered outright by the vampire hunters. Her father had been mortally wounded, but he'd managed to carry the four-year-old Jez to his brother's house before he died. Uncle Bracken had raised her, and he'd told her the story over and over.

But that screaming . . .

It didn't mean anything. It *couldn't*. She was Jez Redfern, more of a vampire than anyone, even Morgead. Of all the lamia, the vampires who could have children, her family was the most important. Her uncle Bracken was a vampire, and so was his father, and his father's father, all the way back to Hunter Redfern.

But her mother . . .

What did she know about her mother's family? Nothing.

Uncle Bracken always just said that they'd come from the East Coast.

Something inside Jez was trembling. She didn't want to frame the next question, but the words came into her mind anyway, blunt and inescapable.

What if her mother had been human?

That would make Jez . . .

No. It wasn't possible. It wasn't just that Night World law forbade vampires to fall in love with humans. It was that there was no such thing as a vampire-human hybrid. It couldn't be *done*; it had never been done in twenty thousand years. Anybody like that would be a freak. . . .

The trembling inside her was getting worse.

She stood up slowly and only vaguely noticed when the skinhead made a sound of fear. She couldn't focus on him. She was staring between the redwood trees.

If it were true . . . it *couldn't* be true, but if it were true . . . she would have to leave everything. Uncle Bracken. The gang.

And Morgead. She'd have to leave Morgead. For some reason that made her throat close convulsively.

And she would go . . . where? What kind of a place was there for a half-human half-vampire freak?

Nowhere in the Night World. That was certain. The Night People would have to kill any creature like that.

The skinhead made another sound, a little whimper. Jez blinked and looked at him.

It couldn't be true, but all of a sudden she didn't care about killing him anymore. In fact, she had a feeling like slow horror creeping over her, as if something in her brain was tallying up all the humans she'd hurt and killed over the years. Something was taking over her legs, making her knees rubbery. Something was crushing her chest, making her feel as if she were going to be sick.

"Get out of here," she whispered to the skinhead.

He shut his eyes. When he spoke it was in a kind of moan. "You'll just chase me."

"No." But she understood his fear. She was a huntress. She'd chased so many people. So many humans . . .

Jez shuddered violently and shut her eyes. It was as if she had suddenly seen herself in a mirror and the image was unbearable. It wasn't Jez the proud and fierce and beautiful. It was Jez the murderer.

I have to stop the others.

The telepathic call she sent out was almost a scream. *Everybody! This is Jez. Come to me, right now! Drop what you're doing and come!*

She knew they'd obey—they were her gang, after all. But none of them except Morgead had enough telepathic power to answer across the distance.

What's wrong? he said.

Jez stood very still. She couldn't tell him the truth. Morgead hated humans. If he even knew what she suspected . . . the way he would look at her . . .

He would be sickened. Not to mention that he'd undoubtedly have to kill her.

I'll explain later, she told him, feeling numb. *I just found out—that it's not safe to feed here.*

Then she cut the telepathic link short. She was afraid he'd sense too much of what was going on inside her.

She stood with her arms wrapped around herself, staring between the trees. Then she glanced at the skinhead, who was still huddled in the sword fern.

There was one last thing she had to do with him.

Ignoring his wild flinching, she stretched out her hand. Touched him, once, on the forehead with an extended finger. A gentle, precise contact.

"Remember . . . nothing," she said. "Now go."

She felt the power flow out of her, wrapping itself around the skinhead's brain, changing its chemistry, rearranging his thoughts. It was something she was very good at.

The skinhead's eyes went blank. Jez didn't watch him as he began to crawl away.

All she could think of now was getting to Uncle Bracken. He would answer her questions; he would explain. He would prove to her that none of it was true.

He'd make everything all right.

J ez burst through the door and turned immediately into the small library off the front hall. Her uncle was sitting there at his desk, surrounded by built-in bookcases. He looked up in surprise.

"Uncle Bracken, who was my mother? How did my parents die?" It all came out in a single rush of breath. And then Jez wanted to say, "Tell me the truth," but instead she heard herself saying wildly, "Tell me it's not true. It's not possible, is it? Uncle Bracken, I'm so scared."

Her uncle stared at her for a moment. There was shock and despair in his face. Then he bent his head and shut his eyes.

"But how is it possible?" Jez whispered. "How am I here?" It was hours later. Dawn was tinting the window. She was sitting on the floor, back against a bookcase, where she'd collapsed, staring emptily into the distance.

"You mean, how can a vampire-human halfbreed exist? I don't know. Your parents never knew. They never expected to have children." Uncle Bracken ran both hands through his hair, head down. "They didn't even realize you could live as a vampire. Your father brought you to me because he was dying and I was the only person he could trust. He knew I wouldn't turn you over to the Night World elders."

"Maybe you should have," Jez whispered.

Uncle Bracken went on as if he hadn't heard her. "You lived without blood then. You looked like a human child. I don't know what made me try to see if you could learn how to feed. I brought you a rabbit and bit it for you and let you smell the blood." He gave a short laugh of reminiscence. "And your little teeth sharpened right up and you knew what to do. That was when I knew you were a true Redfern."

"But I'm not." Jez heard the words as if someone else were speaking them from a distance. "I'm not even a Night Person. I'm vermin."

Uncle Bracken let go of his hair and looked at her. His eyes, normally the same silvery-blue as Jez's, were burning with a pure silver flame. "Your mother was a good woman," he said harshly. "Your father gave up everything to be with her. She wasn't vermin."

Jez looked away, but she wasn't ashamed. She was numb. She felt nothing except a vast emptiness inside her, stretching infinitely in all directions.

And that was good. She never wanted to feel again. Everything she'd felt in her life—everything she could remember—had been a lie.

She wasn't a huntress, a predator fulfilling her place in the scheme of things by chasing down her lawful prey. She was a murderer. She was a monster.

"I can't stay here anymore," she said.

Uncle Bracken winced. "Where will you go?"

"I don't know."

He let out his breath and spoke slowly and sadly. "I have an idea."